PAUL MARGUERITTE

PANTOMIMES
and Other Surreal Tales

Translated and with an introduction by
BRIAN STABLEFORD

PAUL MARGUERITTE (1860-1918) was the older son of General Jean-Auguste Margueritte, who played a leading role in France's colonial conquest of Algeria, where Paul was born. An amateur mime, Paul wrote several pantomimes, most notably *Pierrot assassin de sa femme* (1881), allegedly first performed in Stéphane Mallarmé's salon. In 1885 he published *Tous quatre* (1885), which caused something of a scandal by virtue of its treatment of lesbianism. Margueritte, along with Paul Bonnetain, J. H. Rosny, Lucien Descaves, and Gustave Guiches, released "The Manifesto of the Five" in *Le Figaro* in 1887 attacking the alleged vulgarity and cynical commercialism of Émile Zola's recent novel *La Terre*.

BRIAN STABLEFORD's scholarly work includes *New Atlantis: A Narrative History of Scientific Romance* (Wildside Press, 2016), *The Plurality of Imaginary Worlds: The Evolution of French roman scientifique* (Black Coat Press, 2017) and *Tales of Enchantment and Disenchantment: A History of Faerie* (Black Coat Press, 2019). He has translated more than three hundred volumes from the French, mostly in the genres of *roman scientifique, contes de fées* and Romantic and Symbolist fiction. His recent fiction includes the visionary science fiction novel *The Revelations of Time and Space* (2020) and its sequel *After the Revelation* (2021); the last in his long series of "Tales of the Genetic Revolution," *The Elusive Shadows* (2020); and the comedy fantasy *Meat on the Bone* (2021), all published by Snuggly Books.

CONTENTS

Introduction / *7*
Acknowledgements / *19*

Pantomimes:
  Around the Cat's Neck / *25*
  The Legend of Saint Pierrot / *33*
  Pierrot in love with the Moon / *40*
  Columbine Forgiven / *47*
  Pierrot Dead and Alive / *55*
  Pierrot the Nihilist / *63*
  Pierrot the Mormon / *70*
  Fear / *76*
Dreams and Hauntings:
  The Revenant / *85*
  Sensations of Ether / *92*
  The Pierced Chair / *99*
  The Enchanted Garden / *106*
  Tales for a Rainy Day / *120*
  The Breath / *126*
  The Three Phantoms / *133*

Legends:
    The Stone of the Dwarfs / *143*
    The Sensual Lovers / *150*
    The Red Mountain / *155*
    The Guardian of Bad Dreams / *161*
    The Boat of Porcelains / *168*
The Forest:
    The Dear Forest / *177*
    The Enchanted Forest / *183*
    The Passing Moment / *190*
Ypérion:
    The Mannequin / *199*
    The Adventures of Ypérion / *205*

INTRODUCTION

PAUL MARGUERITTE (1860-1918) was the older son of General Jean-Auguste Margueritte, who played a leading role in France's colonial conquest of Algeria, where Paul was born. In 1870 the general led the Chasseurs d'Afrique in a desperate cavalry charge during the battle of Sedan, in a hopeless attempt to prevent the cornered French Army from being overwhelmed and massacred by Prussian artillery, and he was fatally wounded. Paul's younger brother Victor (1866-1942) initially followed in his father's footsteps, enlisting in the Chasseurs d'Afrique in 1888, but Paul had dedicated himself to a literary vocation as soon as he finished his education, and Victor eventually followed his example, committing himself to it entirely when he resigned his commission in 1896.

Paul's first significant success was a pantomime, *Pierrot assassin de sa femme* (1881), allegedly first performed in Stéphane Mallarmé's salon, which continued a theatrical tradition already thought to be rather *passé*; the role of Pierrot, initially adapted from the Italian *commedia dell'arte*, had been developed independently in Paris by several famous mimes, most notably Jean-Gaspard Deburau (1796-1846), the star of the Théâtre des Funambules. Deburau's Pierrot became an archetypal figure, widely exploited in Romantic art, especially when it gave birth to the Symbolist Movement, where the figure acquired a powerful nostalgia. Théophile Gautier and Charles Baudelaire both waxed enthusiastic about Deburau's Pierrot, and the "Parnassian" poet Théodore de Banville also celebrated his archetypal status. In 1881, Banville, then working for the newspaper *Gil Blas,* was the leading practitioner and chief exemplar of an emergent genre of newspaper short fiction, which increased its appeal and influence slowly over the next decade before becoming a crucially important source of income for French professional writers in the 1890s.

By 1881 the Romantic Movement was also regarded as *passé,* and the attempt to revive and renew it that had been made by the self-styled Parnassians in the inhospitable climate of the Second Empire—during which several of its leading members had been exiled and all of whom were subject to rigorous political censorship—was generally thought to have been a failure. The literary movement newly fashionable after the fall of the Empire was Naturalism, the key manifesto of which had been provided in the late 1860s by Émile Zola, although Zola's combative and rather eccentric prospectus—which represented the Naturalist novel as a quasi-scientific analysis of human nature, providing explanations for human behaviour based in theories of heredity—was opposed by his chief rival practitioners, the more genteel Edmond de Goncourt (1822-1896) and his younger brother Jules (1830-1870).

Paul Margueritte became a regular member of Edmond de Goncourt's weekly salon, known as the *grenier* [grain-loft], and part of a coterie of young writers affiliated with Goncourt's version of the Naturalist creed. Although Zola dropped in on the *grenier* occasionally, to stir the discussion and take advantage of the free cigarettes that Goncourt provided for his guests, his presence always generated a certain tension. One consequence of that tension was the publication in 1887 in the newspaper *Le Figaro*—whose weekly "literary supplement" had been an important model for the literary inclusions of *Gil Blas*—of the "Manifeste des Cinq," in which five young members of Goncourt's coterie, Paul Margueritte, Paul Bonnetain, Lucien Descaves, J. H. Rosny and Gustave Guiches, issued a protest against the alleged vulgarity and cynical commercialism of Zola's recent novel *La Terre* (1887). Goncourt dissociated himself from the *Manifeste*, and most of the members of the group came to regret having written it, but the publicity and the resultant controversy did their careers no harm. Margueritte, Descaves and Rosny were all named in Goncourt's testament along with Joris-Karl Huysmans, Alphonse Daudet and other stalwarts of the *grenier* as prospective members of a committee formed for the purpose of awarding an annual prize to a Naturalist novel, which became known as the "Goncourt Academy."

Paul Margueritte was best known at the time of the *Manifeste*'s publication as the author of a memoir of his father, *Mon père* (1884), and the novel *Tous qua-tre* (1885), which had caused something of a scandal by virtue of its treatment of lesbianism, although the uproar was mild by comparison with the scandals provoked by Bonnetain's *Charlot s'amuse* (1883) and Descaves' *Sous-Offs* (1889). The latter, which led to Descaves' prosecution on a charge of insulting the army, might well have offended Margueritte, given his military connections, but that did not prevent the writers from remaining associated; both of them were recruited by Catulle Mendès, along with Rosny, to join the "stable" of writers providing short fiction regularly to the *Écho de Paris*, which briefly became the leading Parisian market for such work in the early 1890s.

Before being hired by the *Écho* to assemble his stable, Mendès had published short fiction regularly in *Gil Blas* alongside Banville and Armand Silvestre. All three had been associated with the Parnassians in the last days of the Empire, and *Gil Blas* had offered them a golden opportunity to renew careers that were in dire need of a boost. The *Écho* became a significant locus of the last flicker of Romanticism, represented in poetry by the Symbolist Movement, nurtured in the cradle of Stéphane Mallarmé's salon, and Mendès became a significant proponent of Symbolist prose, which lent itself reasonably well to the narrow strait-jacket of newspaper short fiction—but not nearly as well as Naturalism, which was readily adaptable to the anecdotal "slice-of-life" narratives, conversation pieces and character studies that swiftly became the standard formats of newspaper fiction. As the 1890s progressed, those kinds of narrative gradually squeezed more exotic and adventurous fictions out of the regular slots, and after 1900, when the wave of fashionability had broken and newspaper short fiction, where it survived, was moved from prominence on page one to the interior pages, the medium was dominated by formularistic quasi-anecdotal fiction, and remained so during a long aftermath of increasing insignificance.

Initially, Paul Margueritte, although he had been a member of Mallarmé's salon as well as Goncourt's, was one of the more conservative members of the Mendès stable, specializing in anodyne anecdotal stories, but once he settled into the production-line system of delivering a story a week to the *Écho*, the need for a measure of variety led him to experiment more adventurously. As a doctrinaire Naturalist, however, he usually shunned the fantastic intrusions that Mendès was very happy to deploy, even when it became clear that the paper's prosaic bourgeois audience much preferred slightly risqué tales modestly parodying the supposed mores of Parisian high society—in which Mendès also cultivated a considerable expertise. Margueritte was not given to the radical polemicizing of Lucien Descaves, Octave Mirbeau or Jean Richepin, nor to the stylistic flamboyance of Mendès, Marcel Schwob or Jean Lorrain, and many of his stories written for the newspaper were not reprinted in book form, although *Le Cuirassier blanc* (1892) is a significant collection of his earlier stories.

When the core members of the *Écho* stable decamped in 1895 to the pages of *Le Journal*, which took over as the flag-bearer of *fin-de-siècle* short fiction, Margueritte remained loyal to the *Écho*, left behind as one of the leaders of a much-depleted stable, whose most prestigious member was the maverick doyen of Symbolism, Anatole France. In keeping with the general trend, most of Anatole France's regular contributions to the *Écho* in 1896 and thereafter took on a more conventional journalistic form, featuring more non-fiction than fiction, albeit with many hybrid items, and when Paul Margueritte fused his by-line with that of his brother in that year the experimental phase that he had begun in 1894 and continued through 1895 faded out, as they too settled into formularistic repetition, in non-fiction as well as fiction, and in hybridized items. Whereas Anatole France's hybrids tended to take their inspiration from various remote eras of history and legend, however, Paul and Victor Margueritte generally focused narrowly on the events of a single year that loomed large in public memory, and which had a particular significance for them: 1870.

The items in the present volume of translations are all taken from the brief experimental phase of Paul Margueritte's career as a mass-producer of newspaper faction. They include several of his rare forays into weird and supernatural fiction, all of which are tentative and uneasy, but not unenterprising and certainly not uninteresting, plus a few equally-tentative ventures into post-Parnassian prose poetry and allegory. The collection is, however, titled for the most distinctive of his narrative experiments, in which he attempted to adapt the substance of his early pantomimes to the format of short fiction. Some of the resultant stories were also adapted for the stage, notably the last of them, *La Peur* (tr. as *Fear*)—not the only story bearing that title that Margueritte published—which reflected a particular fascination of his, also exhibited in several stories featured in the "Hautings" section of the present volume.

It is arguable that the items in the "Pantomimes" section are unsuccessful as experiments in narrative method, and they certainly seem highly idiosyncratic to the modern eye, but it is worth noting that one of the inevitable corollaries of trying to adapt the art of mime to prose narrative is a conspicuous artificiality that is taken to peculiar extremes in such stories as "Pierrot nihiliste" (tr. as "Pierrot the Nihilist") and "Pierrot Mormon" (tr. as "Pierrot the Mormon"), which entitle Margueritte to be considered an unlikely precursor of Surrealism.

Although all of Paul Margueritte's work between 1896 and 1906 was published under the joint by-line of "Paul and Victor Margueritte," it is probable that most of the items published under that by-line were actually written by one or other brother rather than being combined efforts. The decision to use a joint by-line was undoubtedly partially motivated by the fact that Paul had a contract with the *Écho* to deliver an item every week, and the fusion allowed Victor to relieve him of some of the strain of meeting his deadlines, but there is a more complex historical context to be taken into account, which goes all the way back to the traumatic year of 1870 when—unknown at the time to the ten-year-old Paul—Jules de Goncourt had died.

The Goncourt brothers really had worked in close and intimate collaboration, most famously on their journal, which Edmond published and continued—eventually serialized in the pages of the *Écho*—but which was never quite the same after Jules' death. Edmond's habit of taking young writers under his wing in the *grenier* was seen by several of his contemporaries as a series of attempts to "replace" Jules, and he showed a particular predilection for the Boëx brothers, Joseph and Justin, who decided in the 1890s to share their pseudonym, J. H. Rosny. When Edmond de Goncourt initially wrote his testament, "J. H. Rosny" was the elder brother, but by the time the will was executed, that pseudonym sheltered two people, with the result that both brothers were included in the strictly-limited membership of the "Goncourt Academy," while Edmond's previous leading protégé, Jean Lorrain, was excluded (much to his disappointment). When the will was drafted, Paul Margueritte had not yet formed a close collaboration with Victor, but it was soon before Edmond's death that he did so, and he must have had the example of the Rosnys in mind. He remained close to both Boëx brothers, and eventually died in the home of the younger brother, who had long since quarreled with his elder sibling and had taken to signing his work *J.-H. Rosny jeune* in order to distinguish it from his brother's. It is hard to be sure, but it seems highly probable that very few, if any, of the works signed by the Rosny pseudonym while it was being shared were actually collaborative, and although the Margueritte brothers undoubtedly collaborated closely in the extensive research they did for their historical fiction and non-fiction set in and around 1870, it seems probable that the actual writing was done separately.

Whatever the reasons were for the adoption of joint signatures by the Boëx and Margueritte brothers, however, its aftermath is intriguing. When the Boëx brothers split and divided up their pseudonym the "divorce" was acrimonious. Jules Renard's memoir of the early years of the Goncourt Academy alleged that many of the fierce disputes that notoriously afflicted the debates regarding the annual award of the Prix Goncourt were complicated and fueled by the fact that the younger Rosny insisted on voting against his elder, and that if the elder switched his vote, the younger would do likewise in order to maintain the neutralization. The split between the two Margueritte brothers appears to have been less acrimonious, and could not lead to similar incidental complications because Victor was never admitted to the Goncourt Academy, but again, Paul's awareness of the precedent must have been keen.

Among the first contributions to the *Écho*'s pages bearing the joint by-line of the Margueritte brothers were a series of polemical articles on "*questions feministes*," including a number of studies subsequently collected in *Femmes nouvelles* (1899). The subject was dear to Paul's heart; his marriage had been very unhappy, and had culminated in a separation in 1895, although his attempts to obtain a divorce in court were thwarted; he fled to Algeria with his two daughters after that failure in order to prevent his wife taking custody of them, although he eventually returned to France and made informal arrangements for shared custody. Victor went on, after his brother's death, to obtain a spectacular *succés de scandale* with his novel *La Garconne* (1922; tr. as *The Bacheloress*), which championed a woman's right to the same sexual freedoms tacitly attributed to men, in a deliberately provocative manner.

That sequence of events lends an additional wry significance to the fact that both of Paul's daughters, Eve (1885-1971) and Lucie (1886-1955), who were introduced by their father into Parisian literary society in their teens, and who both signed their work with the improvised surname Paul-Margueritte, became prolific, successful and acclaimed writers. Both married, but Eve was soon widowed and Lucie swiftly divorced, after which the two sisters lived together, and collaborated extensively. Although they used separate by-lines on their fiction, they worked together on numerous translations from English, including classic Naturalist novels by Thomas Hardy and George Gissing, but also Bram Stoker's *Dracula* and a scientific romance by the American astronomer Garrett P. Serviss, *The Second Deluge*.

Paul Margueritte's quasi-anecdotal newspaper fiction includes numerous accounts of childhood, many featuring an eight-year-old boy nicknamed Poum, collected in *Poum, aventures d'un petit garcon* (1897)—*poum* is an onomatopoeia closer in tone to the English *pop* than the direct transcription *boom*)—but also including a parallel and overlapping series featuring a little girl, collected in *Zette* (1900), and girls are more prominent in his numerous stories that take the form of awkwardly whimsical dialogues between adults—often painters, but sometimes writers—and children. Typically eccentric examples included in the present collection include "Sensations d'éther" (tr. as "Sensations of Ether") and "Avenutres d'Ypérion" (tr. as "Ypérion's Adventures"). They were written in a period when the author's relationship with his own young daughters was profoundly problematic, and the shadow cast on his life by his personal problems throughout the 1890s is an obscure presence in most or all of the stories in the collection, contributing significantly to their distinctive ambience. Nowhere is that shadow more obvious than in his pantomime stories, and their sardonic treatment of the perverse and often violent relationship between Pierrot and Columbine

It is arguably no disadvantage to any writer, and a Naturalist writer most of all, to have an unhappy and challenging life, thus to have experience of all the vicissitudes of emotional experience and to draw imaginative and affective fuel therefrom. In spite of the early scandal occasioned by *Tous quatre*, Margueritte was less likely than many of his associates and contemporaries to be criticized and castigated for the alleged "decadence" of his work, but the "morals" of his stories are often a trifle *louche*, and his evident sympathy for the silent and occasionally vicious white-faced Pierrot, equally capable of cruelty and sentimentality, adds a distinctive quality to the character's ever-enigmatic pose. There is a similar elusive quality to many of his other short stories, the more adventurous of which revel in their own idiosyncrasy even when pretending to a strict naturalism and a conventional sentimentality, and are sometimes capable of a casual brutality uncommon even in the cynical medium of the *conte cruel*. The stories assembled in this slim collection fully deserve rescue from their obscure origins, and they benefit from being gathered together—for the first time—into a curious set. They remain intriguingly pointed, more than a century after their composition.

The translations were all made from the copies of *L'Écho de Paris* contained in the Bibliothèque Nationale's archive, reproduced on the *gallica* website.

—Brian Stableford, April 2021.

ACKNOWLEDGEMENTS

All the stories first appeared in *L'Écho de Paris*, on the following dates:

Le Revenant 28 September 1891
Sensations d'éther 7 December 1891
La Chaise percée 3 October 1892
La Pierre des nains 19 December 1892
Le Jardin enchanté 16 & 23 January 1893
Au cou de chat 5 March 1894
Le Mannequin 9 July 1894
La Chère forêt 30 July 1894
La Légende de saint Pierrot 13 August 1894
Pierrot amoureuse de la lune 27 August 1894
Columbine pardonnée 17 September 1894
Pierrot nihiliste 15 October 1894
Pierrot mort et vivant 5 November 1894
Contes d'un jour de pluie 3 December 1894
La Gardienne des mauvais rêves 11 February 1895
Les Voluptueux amants 18 March 1895
Aventures d'Ypérion 8 April 1895
La Forêt fée 13 May 1895

La Montagne rouge 3 August 1895
Pierrot Mormon 7 September 1895
Le Souffle 11 January 1896
Le Bateau de porcelains 21 November 1896*
La Peur 12 December 1896*
L'Heure qui passe 3 April 1897*
Les Trois fantômes 17 June 1897*

Titles marked with an asterisk bore the by-line "Paul et Victor Margueritte."

PANTOMIMES

and Other Surreal Tales

PANTOMIMES

AROUND THE CAT'S NECK

To Comte Primoli[1]

PIERROT'S garden in a summer heat wave. The sky is burning like a sea of alcohol, the sun melting in flames and streaming, the light vibrating in darts, scintillating in feathers and pooling in white sheets on the ground. There is not one leaf that is not sparkling; the sand of the paths is shining like iridescent powdered glass. The warm earth has the odor of hay; a feverish breath is passing over. The thyrses of the hollyhocks rise up like a desire, the poppies are swooning, their mauve, garnet and crimson robes are tucked up all the way to the heart, and the huge hieratic sunflowers are extending their golden mirrors toward the star.

The door of the house opens; Arlequin appears, sinuously. Wearing a mysterious black mask, his figure

---

1 Giuseppe Napoleone (or Joseph Napoléon) Primoli (1851-1927) was a prominent figure in French *fin-de-siècle* high society; in his youth he was at Napoléon III's court, but Théophile Gautier was hired as his tutor and he became an important book-collector, attending Edmond de Goncourt's salon, among others, while dividing his time between Paris and Rome.

molded in green and yellow diamonds whose variegation undulates like the coils of a snake, the shadow of his hat, deployed like a fan, protects the exquisite face of Columbine from the blinding light; she is laughing, having drunk two fingers of champagne at lunch. She is reminiscent of a naked flower; her shoulders and arms are *cuisse-de-nymphe* pink, and so are her legs, under a leotard whose silk is mimicking skin; her bodice is a little cornet of azure, and a gauze skirt, as short as a dancer's, flutters around her with a dragonfly palpitation. The fashion in which she leans on Arlequin's arm and the way their hips brush against one another affirm the delightful hypocrisy of adulterous intimacy. Her husband, Pierrot, follows in his white smock, carrying a tray on which coffee cups clink. Behind him, with a velvet tread and its tail erect, glides Mime, Columbine's black kitten, which collects itself, bristling, alternately arching its back like a dromedary and stretching like a clawed hare.

In the arbor where they sit down the shade is exquisite. A tangle of verdure mingling convolvulus, nasturtiums and sweet peas filters the light delicately, and smells good. Pierrot drinks his coffee blissfully, into which Columbine dips a sugar-lump, while Arlequin smokes a fat cigar. The kitten licks its paw, polishes the end of its nose with it, and goes to bite a flea on its backside. Columbine falls upon it, picks it up, rolls it into a ball, wrings it like a cloth, and folds it in various manners, all horrifying for Mime, who wriggles. She covers it with passionate kisses, cradles it in her arms, calls it by the most endearing names, puts it around her neck like a fur stole, nests it in the hollow of her breasts, where the rice-powder makes it sneeze, and finally hooks it on to Pierrot's hat. He jumps and struggles under the scratches. Mime flees, mewling, horribly vexed.

Columbine bursts into laughter. In a frolicsome mood, she pirouettes, her fingers sketching a waltz on an imaginary piano; she spots a rope extended between two trees and unties it in order to skip with it like a little girl. *To you, Pierrot, Arlequin: take one end each!* She gets ready, already leaping. A flick of the wrist, the rope goes *dzz* and Columbine sets off. Clumsy fools! They have whipped her ankle. She bounds again, and falls. That's their fault too; they don't know how to twirl! A further attempt, also unsuccessful. Chagrined, she snatches the rope from their hands and goes to skip on her own. Arlequin returns to his cigar and Pierrot, in order to savor the spectacle, lies down on his back in the best part of the flower bed. A greedy expectation raises his eyebrows like circumflex accents and his mouth rounds out like an O while his gaze climbs along the tapering legs.

"Imbecile!" she says; and, shrugging her shoulders, she stiffens the rope and launches herself, her knees tucked up like a circus rider. At each jump her skirt inflates, flattens and puffs up like whipped cream; sunlight zigzags the curves of her ankles, and her arms, rotating very rapidly, uncover the down of a blonde bird in the hollow of a nest, which the black kitten, duped thereby, watches carefully as it approaches gradually, fascinated, with cruelty in its pale green eyes.

Columbine throws one of her slippers at its nose, and then the other, amused by Mime's mad pursuit of the pink fabric, and, as she does not want, thus rendered barefoot, to step on little stones, she comes down, feet together, on Pierrot's chest. There, entirely at ease on the living trampoline, without interrupting her cadence, she jumps, jumps again and keeps on jumping within the golden circle of the luminous rope. One might think that she were dancing in her own aureole. And, light as she is, Pierrot, whom she tramples underfoot, experiences the pangs of an exquisite martyrdom.

"Again!" he cries, with tears in his eyes, his ribs cracking. She, however, smiles with a triumphant perversity at Arlequin, whose eyes light up behind the mask, his canine teeth bristling in a smile that would like to kiss and bite. It is for him that she is dancing so lasciviously, a funambulesque Salome, and the gleams cast by her jewelry—a diamond comb, a pearl necklace, golden rings and bracelets—are fulgurant sparks that envelop her with stars.

Arlequin, fearing that she might tire herself out, plucks the pink slippers from the cat's teeth and presents them to Columbine, whose big toe he kisses while kneeling, forcing her to lean on his shoulder in order not to lose her equilibrium, while Pierror serves as a floor.

Mime, unfortunately, has approached too closely. She picks the kitten up, and, in a surge of furious tenderness, juggles with it, throwing it up like a ball and catching it again. Then, sitting down under the arbor, for the amusement of her husband and her lover, she takes pleasure in trying her rings on the kitten's paws.

Because it stretches its digits and contracts its claws, none of them will fit. Perhaps a collar would suit it better. She slips a bracelet from her arm, laughing at the idea of putting it around Mime's neck. She tries, in spite of the kitten's protestations. She forces its head into the circle of gold constellated by brilliants, which is already making it a chin-strap and flattening its ears.

Pierrot becomes alarmed. "Look out!"

Arlequin also exclaims: "Stop!"—not out of pity for the kitten, which might be strangled, but because the necklace, once dug into the flesh, might not emerge again. Both of them calculate the circumference of the cat's neck and the swelling of its head The gold bracelet will certainly not be able to pass back!

Columbine makes fun of their dread; the risk of the game is tempting in itself; the desperation of Mime, who goes *Pfft! Pfft!* and bristles, excites her. She forces it—but scarcely is the cat's neck encircled than, adorned with the narrow jewel, it leaps like a carp, clawing tight and left, and disappears, mewling funereally, over the wall at the end of the garden.

The despairing Columbine cries: "My bracelet! My beautiful bracelet! Stop, thief! Stop, thief!"

Pierrot murmurs, seductively: "Here, Mimi! Here, little Mimi! Here, my friend!"

Arlequin makes the gesture of raising a rifle to his shoulder, his mouth bursts forth: "*Poum!*" and he leaps up in order to go and fetch a weapon, while Columbine laments more loudly.

"Oh, catch him! My bracelet, which I loved so much, my pretty bracelet! Vile tomcat! Horrible beast! After the cat! After the cat!"

Pierrot puts a hand over her mouth, retaining Arlequin with the other by the hem of his trousers. If they make so much noise, Mime won't come back. It's necessary to hold a council and deliberate.

"What if we were to arm the peasants and beat the bushes, with bloodhounds and officers on horseback?" suggests Arlequin.

"What if we were to put a price on his head and a reward for whoever brings the necklace back?" proposes Columbine.

Pierrot smiles thinly. He will think of something better. They can take a live mouse from the mousetrap. Drawing the other two along, he matches speech with action, attaches a string to the mouse's paw and the string to a fishing rod. Taking the whole behind the wall, they hide there. Arlequin and Columbine agitate their handkerchiefs at the top while the mouse is released on the string. It runs along the wall, going up and down and dancing like a hook on the end of the line.

Holding their breath, their hearts palpitating, wide-eyed, waving their white handkerchiefs like the wings of doves, they hear an ungraspable friction, the approach of a dwarf tiger in the jungle of grass. Look out! Prudently, Pierrot brings back the mouse at the end of the line; a head with green eyes and a golden necklace around the neck falls over the wall with a single bound. Six hands close upon it!

Mime is captured. The mouse gnaws through the string and runs away. The joy of the three accomplices is manifest in a jig, brief but expressive, and within the clenched cluster of their hands the cat, pulled this way and that, risks being torn apart.

"A prisoner! What luck! Surrender the necklace, tomcat."

But what has been foreseen transpires; the bracelet can no longer be extracted; the head will be torn off sooner. Pierrot pulls in vain while the others stretch the cat in the opposite direction. They can inflict torture upon it, but the necklace will not budge. What to do? Saw through the gold of the bracelet? Soap Mime's head to make it slippery? Shut the poor thing in a box and let it starve until the necklace falls from its neck? Or else . . . an atrocious idea that Arlequin sketches with a trenchant gesture of a guillotine?

Columbine weeps. Pierrot turns his face away.

It's necessary to do something, though, and quickly. If Mime succeeds in running away again, all will be lost. To decapitate it with a single blow, my God! If they were sure of not making it suffer too much . . . well, who can tell? On reflection, will that diabolical vision seduce Columbine? An exquisite and frightful smile twists her lips into a bow, and her face, from which the shadow of sad clouds flees, is brightened by sunlight. Her feverish hands demand her bracelet, already recovering and caressing it, wanting to have it at any price. Arlequin, who has disappeared, brings a hatchet and a wooden block from the kitchen. The frightful solemnity of death hovers in the air.

"Mercy!" begs Pierrot.

"My bracelet!" demands Columbine.

Modesty demands that she retire, at least, but she intends to see, to touch, to sniff. It is her who addresses to the once-adored kitten a pathetic adieu, who kisses it on the eyelids and exhorts it to die well. It is her who maintains it, with all her strength, on the wooden block, where Mime palpitates and gasps; she waits and watches, her nostrils quivering, frightened and delighted.

Pierrot blocks his ears and weeps, his face veiled by his sleeves. Arlequin, the executioner, raises the hatchet, braces himself and relaxes; there is a hideous dull thud. The cat's head flies off like a champagne cork and the necklace, launched around a crimson jet, goes to roll on the bloody ground.

Columbine picks it up; murderous gleams of lust and avid possession burn in her eyes; perversely sensual laughter shakes her; she agitates the streaming red bracelet, and wipes it on Pierrot's immaculate white blouse. He recoils, rowing with his arms, in horror.

THE LEGEND OF SAINT PIERROT[1]

IN the middle of a landscape of rocks, a cavern gapes. At the back, a bed of dry leaves is distinguishable, a couch and a stool. On the latter is a folio Bible surmounted by a loaf of bread pierced by a knife. At the foot of the stool a death-head is sniggering. A spade leaning against the wall emits a livid blue gleam.

It is still daylight.

The drama opens in this fashion:

Kneeling, with his hands joined, Saint Pierrot, his head aureoled and wearing a monk's habit, is praying. His lips are moving, outlining *paters* and *oremuses*. He is thin, sad and disabused. His eyes look up, white with hope, and fall back, somber and discouraged. He makes the sign of the cross and gets to his feet.

---

1 Fake legends of the saints became a significant subgenre of stories featured in the *Écho de Paris*, exemplified by Catulle Mendès series of parodic "*légendes tendres.*" Mendès had also produced a series of "*pantomimes heroiques,*" some of them featuring Pierrot. The most famous modern version of the legend of Saint Anthony, parodied here, was by Gustave Flaubert, but an important variant of it had recently been produced by Margueritte's colleague in the *Écho* stable, Anatole France, in *Thaïs* (1890).

Let's go to work, he mimes. *Let's dig our ditch. I'll soon be at rest, being old.*

He digs momentarily, and then wipes the sweat from his brow, wearily.

I'm thirsty. Let's drink.

But as soon as the pitcher approaches his lips, he sets it aside.

No, it's necessary not to drink with sensuality, but rather seriously, with indifference.

He drinks and sets down the pitcher.

It's only water. Wine would be better. And to eat? I haven't touched that bread yet today.

He cuts a slice and sniffs it.

That's bad. It's necessary not to sniff. Fresh cheese, though . . . that's a nice odor! No, it's bad. I eat too quickly. One more mouthful! The sin of gluttony!

He puts down his unfinished slice of bread.

To nourish the heart and brain, let's read the Bible!

He picks up the folio and opens it at random after having sat down.

That's good, it's fine, it's good, it's satisfying, it's . . . um . . . a little boring.

He yawns, nods his head and goes to sleep. A snore wakes him up. He starts.

Let's read another passage; there are amusing ones.

He leafs through the pages rapidly, squinting his eyes and mouth; a little laugh runs through his body: the drunkenness of Noah, Lot's daughters . . . ha ha! The Bible falls. Terrified, he picks it up, and, throwing himself to his knees: *Pardon me, Lord! Peccavi! Confiteor!*

He strikes his breast.

What's the matter with me today?

He perceives the death's-head and adopts an expression of lofty meditation, index finger in the air.

Ah, how intently it stares at me! How it sniggers!

He picks it up.

To think that I shall be like that! Yes!

He feels the bones beneath his skin.

There are the temples, the nape of the neck, the orbits, the holes of the nose, the jaw. That's scarcely beautiful. Well, why are you looking at me like that?

He is distressed by the grimaces of the death's-head.

Get away, billiard ball!

He throws it away and looks around.

Always alone. No one to say bonjour to. How bored I am!

He stretches his arms despairingly.

However. I'm a man. If I had . . . I'd like, yes . . . to see a beautiful woman, to declare my tenderness to her, to kneel before her, to embrace her, at the risk of my damnation. Ah . . . !

He looks around.

Nothing, no one . . . how depressing!

He weeps.

A very old pilgrim, tall and white-bearded, arrives along a narrow path through the rocks. Stooped, exhausted and tremulous, he is leaning on a curved staff.

Saint Pierrot perceives him and pretends, hypocritically, to be saying his rosary. There is an exchange of civilities.

"I'm hungry and thirsty," says the pilgrim.

Pierrot offers him what he has: water and bread.

The disgusted pilgrim throws away what is offered to him. Saint Pierrot enters into a terrible rage and raises his arm to strike him. *Clash of cymbals!* The habit and beard of the old man fall and in his place there is Columbine, half-naked, a flower of flesh in a pink silk robe.

"Horror!" exclaims Pierrot. He recoils. "Don't touch me! *Vade retro, Satanas!*"

He covers up his eyes, nose and ears, but Columbine sketches a seductive dance. She takes him successively by the five senses; one after another, he reopens his eyes, nose and ears, pulls his tongue desirously, palpates his nostrils and agitates his curled fingers. He embraces her and falls at her feet. She bursts out laughing and, mocking him, escapes him. He runs after her right away, protesting by means of a great oath that he adores her. She pretends to doubt it.

"What about your aureole, then?" she mimes.

He tears it away.

"Stamp on it!"

He stamps on it.

"And the habit?"

He tears it off, becoming Pierrot again, naked and white; his habit, thrown into the nettles, is engulfed by a trapdoor from which a flame emerges.

And now, Pierrot mimes, enlacing the woman, *come!*

He draws her toward the bed of leaves. She lies down; her head is too low. He brings her the folio Bible. She makes a pillow of it.

Pierrot arranges everything for their wedding night, encountering the death's head, which makes him shudder. With a mighty kick, he sends it into the wings. He is prostrating himself, piously, at Columbine's feet when he is stopped, petrified, by a hallucination.

Dusk has fallen; night is commencing. Moonlight throws a white curtain over the wall of rocks, and on that luminous sheet, colored Chinese shadows, painted by Willette,[1] which represent the future, are outlined and file past:

Firstly, Pierrot and Columbine enlaced.

Then Columbine trailing a fat abdomen.

Then Columbine writhing in a great maternal spasm.

Further on, she is nursing her child, and other children.

And Pierrot and Columbine walking—old, ugly and deformed, toward the grave.

Then come their children, a pullulating family, a procession terminated by monsters, hunchbacks and cripples.

Everything fades away; the white sheet becomes dark; the moon is hidden. Pierrot shivers with horror. He repudiates that carnal marriage, the material joy that awaits him, hazardous and bestial fecundity.

He goes to kill Columbine, in order to have her Soul. That Soul he could love and possess in confidence and security.

He arms himself with the long bread knife and strikes Columbine at the moment when she stands up,

---

1 Presumably the British painter Arthur Willett (1857-1918), best known for his water-color landscapes.

her two arms extended in terror. She collapses like a rag, uttering a terrible scream.

Her Soul flies away from that human mannequin.

Where has she gone? A fire follet, the gleam of a gauze skirt, a fluid scintillation, she comes and goes, approaching and drawing away, as if plaintive. Pierrot, desperately, frantically, evokes that Soul, conjures her with all the force of his will.

She reappears, indecisive at first, under superimposed gauzes, gradually becomes precise, and individualizes in a milky moonbeam.

Pierrot declares his tenderness to her. He tries to seize her, but she always escapes him. He becomes desolate, and laments. She reflects and mimes his gestures exactly, seeming to be an echo depicting his pain.

He moves away; she follows him. He runs away; she pursues him. He runs after her but she escapes.

He offers her wild roses and some gold that he has hidden. She shakes her head. What would she do with them? A Soul does not feel anything or enjoy anything. Pierrot touches her, caresses her and hugs her in vain; she melts in his hands. He could palpate Columbine, the flower of flesh, but he cannot grasp her spiritualized twin; that phantom has no gauze corolla. She goes away, fatigued.

"Stay!" he implores.

She comes back.

Ah! he mimes. *If I kill myself, and my Soul will be united with her Soul.*

She smiles, invitingly. He gives himself a great blow with the knife. He extends his weakening arms toward

Columbine's Soul, and tastes atrocious disappointment, the horrible stupor of seeing her slowly escape
him and vanish, volatilized: a breath, a spirit, a dead
gleam.

She vanishes and he falls dead, convulsed, his fingers curled like claws.

Snow falls, the muzzles of jackals are profiled behind
the rocks, with their eyes shining. A large crow, wings
extended, alights on the red wound in his side through
which Saint Pierrot is bleeding. The snow intensifies;
the wind laments; and the curtain comes down.

PIERROT IN LOVE WITH THE MOON

To Elémir Bourges[1]

THE scene passes in a Watteau park bathed in moonlight. Quincunxes and hornbeam hedges. Magical mist. The moon, full and round, in the center of the stage, is reflected in a blue-tinted pond overhung by a white balustrade. In the foreground, to the right, is an altar to Amour, garlanded with roses, bathes in the moonlight. On the pedestal, the statue of the infant Amour, armed with a bow and quiver, with two little wings on his back, is outlined in white and pink against the pale sky.

---

1 Elémir Bourges (1852-1925) was to be a winner of the Prix Goncourt and was subsequently elected as a member of the Goncourt Academy, although he had accused Naturalists of having belittled and deformed humanity. Some critics would undoubtedly have said the same about his notorious novel *Le Crépuscule des dieux*, (1884), which describes a decadent aristocratic family given to overweening pride and incest.

I

Pierrot arrives at a run, as if pursued. He is wearing, not the floating cotton sackcloth of Deburau but the slightly clinging garment of the jolly Gilles,[1] with the floury make-up as well, beneath the headband and small hat. He is fleeing Columbine, like an importunate wasp, whose buzz he is imitating; thus she is harassing him. Does she not think that he is crazy, because he is in love with the Moon? And why should he not be? She is so beautiful, very round, very smooth, very bright, as pure as a lily, as splendid as a rose. He falls into contemplation before her and admires her ecstatically.

He sings her a ballad.

He consecrates a prayer to her, on his knees.

He appeals to her and makes all kinds of enticing gestures. He implores her . . . Nothing!

He tries to go to her, since she will not come to him. A skiff is moored to the bank of the pond. He gets into it and raises his arms toward the Moon; he risks capsizing. He climbs on to the balustrade and falls off. He tries to seize her in the water, where her reflection is laid out, in order to kiss her and take her, face down over the water. He only succeeds in wetting his fingers and getting a mouthful of water, which makes him sneeze like a sprinkled cat.

---

1 Gilles was a stock character of eighteenth-century French farce and pantomime, a clone of Pierrot who lost his fashionability when Deburau revamped the Italianate original. He figures in a famous painting by Jean-Antoine Watteau (1684-1721), inventor of the *fête galante* genre of paintings, echoed in countless stage sets.

Columbine arrives, in a striped skirt and lilac scarf. She reproaches Pierrot bitterly. Why is he fleeing her? Her, who cares for him so much, who makes him such nice little dishes! Has he forgotten the chops turning on the spit, the massive hams, the eggs delicately broken in omelets? And the sweet wines that warm him, the champagne that bubbles and foams? She herself is the most succulent meal of all, does he not care about her? However . . . and she looks at her breasts, like doves with pink beaks, her round and slender thighs, and sketches a swing of her hips that makes her skirt swell.

Pierrot remains insensible.

Oh, in that case, she threatens him, she will leave him for Arlequin, the multicolored flutterer.

Pierror remains cold.

In that case, she will cheat on him with a captain with a curly moustache and a belly like a beer barrel, from which gold coins tumble.

Pierrot shrugs his shoulders.

She mimes despair: "All right; I'll kill myself."

"Good," says Pierrot, and encourages her to do it. "What will you use? A knife, a rope, fire or poison?"

"Oh," cries Columbine, "how unfortunate I am! All because of that Moon—that plaster mask with which you're in love; that accursed, frightful, decrepit old Moon! Oh, the horror!"

And she shows her fist to her rival and spits into the pond, on the Moon in the water. The indignant Pierrot threatens her, but she laughs at him. He pursues her. She runs away and hides behind Amour's altar.

III

Pierrot comes back, out of breath after his vain run. He proffers vague threats against the invisible Columbine, and in his breathlessness he lies down on a flowery bank and falls asleep.

IV

Columbine emerges from behind the altar. She is desperate, because she loves Pierrot. In her despair, she takes off her scarf in order to hang herself. When she turns round she perceives the infant Amour standing above the altar and runs to kneel down before him; she implores him ardently.

Amour emerges from his immobility, becomes animate, smiles, stretches himself, changes his pose and recites a couplet:

"Since you've always served me well and Pierrot has forsaken you, I'll give you the means to punish him. He prefers the Moon to you, not knowing that that amour is insensate. Amuse yourself with him, and be changed, in order to cure him, into

the Fay of the Moon!"

Clash of cymbals! Columbine's dress falls; she appears as the first quarter of the moon, and runs, clad in blue gauze sparkling with gems, with a luminous crescent in her hair. Her face, her arms and her long legs have the bright pallor of the star.

The nocturnal light has faded.

The full moon in the sky, by virtue of an effect of transparency, is reduced to a crescent.

A scherzo sighs.

And it is spring.

V

Pierrot wakes up and admires the fay of the Moon, dazzled. What—it's her! Yes, it's her, in person, descended to earth. And she dances, symbolizing the youth of the Moon and her own youth. Pierrot tries to seize her, but, virginal, she escapes him with nimble leaps and opposes him, like a roebuck, with the tip of the luminous crescent pinned in her hair, by which he is scratched.

Clash of cymbals!

The fay of the Moon changes into a full moon, and on her forehead a diamante disk, substituted for the crescent, evokes the full Moon. In the sky, similarly, the crescent has become an orb. An andante rises. It is summer. It is very bright. A dance, all lasciviousness and languor; it is the maturity of the Moon, the Moon-woman that Pierrot wants to clasp in his arms; but, being icy, she chills him. *Brr!*

Clash of cymbals!

The fay of the Moon metamorphoses; on the forehead she longer bears anything but a pale crescent; her hair has gone gray, powdered by age. The Moon in the sky is no longer anything more than a meager quarter. It is dark. An adagio sighs; it is autumn. The fay's dance expresses it; it is the autumn of the Moon and the autumn of the woman. And Pierrot feels sad and disabused, like her, all of whose gestures reject him in a melancholy fashion.

Clash of cymbals!

The moon has disappeared. It is pitch dark. It is winter. It is snowing. There is no longer a crescent on the forehead of the discrowned fay, who, in the darkness, over the lamentation of a scherzo, draws away, almost invisible, and disappears from the gaze of the motionless and disappointed Pierrot.

VI

Dawn breaks, cold and sad.

Pierrot rubs his eyes. Has he been dreaming? He feels bleak. The morning cold stings him. All sorts of bourgeois reflections assail him. With Columbine, he would be warm in his house, eating well and drinking better. What about love? Here, he is freezing. Is that reasonable? He no longer loves the Moon at all. Furthermore, it's raining and windy. And Columbine? Where has she been? To find Arlequin again? The Captain? The Banker? Has she killed herself? Yes, probably. It's all over; nothing remains but to hang himself.

And, spotting Columbine's scarf, he makes a slip knot and looks for a tree in order to suspend himself from it by the neck.

Then Amour, on his altar, extends his arm, and in a little couplet he reproaches Pierrot for his inconstancy. It was him, Amour, who changed Columbine into the fay of the Moon, in order to cure Pierrot. If Pierrot promises to be good, he will return her to him.

Columbine reappears, in her striped skirt, with her smiling face, white breasts and round calves.

"Love her henceforth!" orders Amour.

Passionate oaths on Pierrot's part. Amour blesses the enlaced couple.

Fireworks.

COLUMBINE FORGIVEN

To Mlle Peppa Invernizzi[1]

THE scene is a garret. On a table, there is a large knife stuck in a loaf of bread and an empty bottle. In a corner, an old chest. Above it, a portrait of Columbine. At the back of the room, behind slightly-parted red curtains, is a bed alcove without a sheet, whose torn mattress is losing its stuffing. Through an open window, falling snow can be seen. A cuckoo clock on the wall marks the hour.

---

1 The Milanese actress Peppina, or Peppa, Invernizzi (c1840-c1900) was, for a while, a star of the Paris Opéra, who worked there in the latter part of her career as a mime, playing Pierrot in *Le Docteur blanc* (1893) by Catulle Mendès, where the character murders his wife, much as in Margueritte's first pantomime. Mendès' pantomime stories for the *Écho* included versions of his own stage farces and he dedicated the published version of his libretto for Gabriel Pierné's *Le Collier de saphirs* (1892) to "Mademoiselle Peppa Invernizzi."

I

Pierrot is visible, slumped on a chair, his elbows on the table and his head in his hands; the empty bottle and the big knife loom over him. Tallow is running from a poor candle. The music of Paul Vidal[1] is echoing, to a faint rhythm, the sadness of the snow and the end of the carnival.

Pierrot, who is cold, raises his head, shivers, warms his numb fingers at the candle, twists his arms desperately in the solitude, looks at the portrait of the absent Columbine, and curses her. She has deceived him. He found her here, in the bed, naked, in the arms of a man, who ran away after a fight. He has thrown her out too, into the street. Since then, he has missed her. Oh, if she would come back, he would forgive her! Melancholy rises within him, and to the tune of a slow waltz, he takes a beloved garment out of the old chest along with a broken fan, a flower and a little shoe, and then throws them away. What to do? Alas! Alone . . . always alone. He will not drink; he has drunk too much, until he feels sick, on so many evenings. He will try to sleep. Not in the adulterous bed—oh, the disgust!—but there, on the chest. He lets himself fall on to it, his back to the wall. Gradually, his head nods, his eyes blink, his arm swings like a pendulum and then stops. Slumber, forgetfulness and death.

---

1 The composer and music teacher Paul Vidal (1863-1931) often conducted the orchestra at the Opéra in the 1890s; he provided incidental music there for plays by Théodore de Banville and Catulle Mendès.

II

Knock, knock, knock on the door; gently, then more forcefully. Swathed in a hooded mantle scattered with snow, a woman slips in stealthily. She throws back her somber mantle and appears, naked under gauze, dazzling in her new dress and her jewels, diamonds and gold: Columbine!

"Oh, Pierrot!"

She approaches and examines him.

"How he has aged, how empty he is! Poor, poor Pierrot!" Yes, she recognizes everything: the bed, the cuckoo clock (an association of ideas that makes her smile, the slut!)—the bed (A new vicious suggestion; she laughs, the wretch!). But she is hungry and thirsty. What does he have that is good? The bread? Pooh! How stale and moldy it is! That bottle? It's empty and acidic. Pierrot drinks to forget, that's obvious. She examines him again.

"Ah, he's dreaming; he's smiling. What will he say when he wakes up? Bah! He'll take hold of me, caress me, ask for my forgiveness. Oh! His dreams are darkening, his face is becoming nasty. What if he were to throw me out again, or beat me?"

Then she notices the knife stuck in the bread, the big knife, and is struck by a thought.

"What if he were going to . . . with that . . . in my bare breast! No! I'm afraid . . . I'm going away."

She envelops herself rapidly in her mantle and makes as if to leave. But . . .

Pierrot wakes up and overtakes her, in a stupor of a poorly dissipated nightmare. Who is she? What does she want? Let her speak—he wishes it.

She uncovers her face. Tableau. Silence.

"Go away!" says Pierrot.

He goes to open the door wide.

"Go away!" He makes a grand gesture of exile.

"But look, it's so cold out. It's snowing. Have pity!"

"That's true; it's too cold. Stay."

"Thank you." She tries to kiss Pierrot's hand. He snatches it away and wipes it. "Don't touch me!"

She draws away.

She draws away and looks at him, meditating seduction. The seduction commences immediately, to the rhythm of a catchy, dolorous and sensual waltz, a waltz that enlaces the heart, charms the memory, recalls old kisses, promises others, and gradually extracts forgiveness.

There is a slow extension toward Pierrot of hands, eyes and lips. Every time, when he senses her near him, warm and naked, he chases her away. But every time she comes back, touches him, and, his hatred fading away, bitter desire takes him by the throat. His nostrils palpate, his hands tremble. On his face, as pale as death, a horrible expression emerges of regret, despair and amour. Columbine envelops him, presses him, seizes his hands, knots them around her waist, draws him toward her, lifts herself up to him, offers him her lips, and over a crystalline scale, in which Vidal's music palpitates like a sob, the final kiss, marrying the mouths, explodes.

Columbine is triumphant; her laughter bursts forth.

"Ah!" says Pierrot. "You're laughing; me, I'm weeping. Tears have traced furrows in my cheeks. You've sold yourself! Your dress, your bracelets . . . ! Ah, prostitute!"

He raises his arm to strike her.

"You've forgiven me," the enchantress replies. "Look at me; I'm so beautiful."

"Oh," deplores Pierrot, "beautiful . . . too beautiful . . . so beautiful! I no longer have any courage, you've captured me. I'm a coward; people will trample me underfoot like something spat out. You're mine, let's love one another!"

He draws her toward him; she defends herself.

"Come, I want you!" And the flame of rape passes through his eyes. She struggles and tears herself away from him, with a cry of pain, showing him her bruised hand.

"You've hurt me!"

"Forgive me!" he begs,

"Get down in your knees, then!"

He kneels.

"Flat on your belly."

He hesitates.

"Flat on your belly!"

He lies down.

She puts her foot on the nape of his neck and exults, triumphantly, at his debasement.

But the cuckoo in the clock grates, opens its little door, flaps its wings and sings: "Cuckoo! Cuckoo!"

Columbine laughs. Pierrot gets up and puts his hands around her neck.

"What if I strangle you?"

"Do it, then!" and she extends her beautiful neck.

He looks at her, his fingers clenched on her flesh, very gently, and then, fascinated, he lowers his eyes and loosens the murderous grip, sighing: "I can't."

She touches his forehead. "Poor fool!"

"Oh! Yes, very foolish. My reason has fled. And he follows the flight of the disappeared bird with his gaze.

"I'm going to sleep," says Columbine. "I'm tired. Good night!"

"Together?" says Pierrot.

"No, alone."

"Pity!"

"You can sleep there." She shows him the chest.

"Columbine!"

"Adieu."

And slowly, to the languid rhythm of the music, she disappears behind the curtain.

IV

Alone, Pierrot passes his hand over his forehead, trying to think.

She's there, there! She's undressing, taking off her stockings, her corset. It's her who betrayed him, who will betray him again, and always!

How pale he is, in the mirror! Why so pale? And his gaze goes toward the large knife planted in the bread.

The knife attracts him magnetically.

No, oh, no! The horror! He doesn't want to.

The knife attracts him!

Perrot turns round and draws away, with his hands repelling the temptation.

The knife attracts him!

Walking backwards, Pierrot draws nearer.

The knife attracts him!

He wipes sweat away from his brow, shaking away the droplets, throws himself on the implement, brandishes it, hypnotizing himself by mirroring his eye in the trenchant blade; then, stiffly, turning round with a slow and somnambulistic rigidity, he runs and disappears behind the curtains, which fall back, palpitating with the terrible agitation of a struggle.

A cry, like that of an animal having its throat cut, howling.

Pierrot reappears, haggard. His knife is red and dripping. He has blood on his white blouse. He throws the weapon down and opens the curtains wide. Columbine is visible, lying across the bed, with one leg dangling lasciviously—dead. Oh, so beautiful, her heart pierced, all red! Oh, so sweet, her hair hanging down! Oh, so terrible, her eyes revulsed, her tongue in the corner of her mouth!

Pierrot leans over, takes her head and kisses her lips. The head falls back. Plop! Pierrot draws away slowly and reaches the door, his face turned toward the dead woman, to the faint sound of the music that is symbolizing the end of the carnival and the sadness of the snow.

Curtain.

PIERROT DEAD AND ALIVE

To Léon Hennique[1]

I

IN a sickroom, on a night-table, there are medicinal phials of all sizes. There is a pierced chair in a corner, and horse-syringes.[2] Pierrot is dying. A nurse is snoring in a comfortable armchair after having stuffed herself with *ris de veau*. Agitated by nervous tremors. Pierrot is pulling dolorous faces, his staring eyes shining desperately.

---

1 Léon Hennique (1850-1935) was a Naturalist novelist and playwright, a friend of Émile Zola until they fell out over the Dreyfus affair. As one of the executors of Edmond de Goncourt's will, he was instrumental in the founding of the Goncourt Academy, which first met at his house. His work for the stage included the pantomime *Pierrot sceptique* (1881), written in collaboration with Joris-Karl Huysmans. His daughter Nicolette (1882-1956) became a Symbolist poet.

2 A *syringe de cheval*, here translated literally as "horse-syringe" was a large device that was indeed used for administering medicaments to horses, but was also used to introduce liquids into the human gut, at either end.

He tries in vain to wake the nurse, and then tips over a chair under her nose. She starts, sneezes and stuffs her nose with snuff.

What does Pierrot want?

To confess. Quickly, a priest!

He shall have one. The old woman goes out; and Columbine appears.

Well dressed, in tulle, very gracious, with her eternal smile, her large bright eyes unconscious, she advances delighted with her purchases. An employee of the Bon Marché follows her and unpacks various trinkets and frilly satin garments. She pays him and says bonjour to her husband. He listens avidly. He's a dear! And she turns back to her purchases, admiring them.

The doctor arrives. He salutes, ausculates Pierrot, sniffs him and shakes him.

"Oh, the hearty fellow, there's nothing wrong with him, nothing at all."

He scribbles a prescription, smiles at Columbine and says to her: "He's doomed."

Columbine shrugs her shoulders behind the doctor's back as he leaves. Pierrot very ill? Get away! She goes to tickle him. He laughs. There! It's nothing at all. She knows that. And, having other purchases to make, she leaves.

Pierrot smiles; two tears run down his cheeks. He is abandoned.

The priest comes in, followed by the aged nurse. He sits down comfortably. They are left alone. The confession escapes the lips of the moribund. The priest takes an extreme interest in it. Something makes him laugh, something else astonishes him; he criticizes it. Suddenly, indignation carries him away; he throws himself on Pierrot and rains blows upon him; then, very calmly, he gives him absolution and leaves.

The daylight is fading. Pierrot recovers consciousness. The solitude frightens him. He raises himself on his elbow, tries to get up, and falls back, more than once. His death-throes commence, while two white butterflies, having entered through the window, embroider their amorous frolics to the accompaniment of a funeral march.

Pierrot gasps, his breast hollows out and his heart stops. Only his hands are alive, groping in the void. Suddenly, his eyes revulse, and the butterflies fly away from the corpse.

II

The day of the burial; relatives and guests are there, very bored. Hands are shaken, there are yawns as if to dislocate jaws. Columbine, dressed in mourning, is sobbing. A man of the world—or rather *the* Man of the World—a veritable picture of concern, hastens around her. The cadaveric Pierrot cuts out a rigid profile at the back of the alcove. Meanwhile, plates of food are passed round, ladies munch éclairs and swill glasses of redcurrant syrup.

The undertakers enter, in a hurry, jostling everyone. The concerned Monsieur takes the tearful Columbine away. Here comes the bier. One, two, plop! Pierrot is dumped; an imperceptible shudder—of pain?—passes over the dead man's face. He is nailed under the coffin lid. It is lifted up. Columbine is sobbing on the arm of the increasingly gallant Monsieur. "Whenever you please, Messieurs!" says the master of ceremonies.

III

Uncertain moonlight bathes high cemetery walls with dazzling whiteness. Pierrot's tomb, brand new, has the raw whiteness of plaster. Wreaths strew it, which agitate, to the sound of a shrill and hasty music. The iron cross falls, the tombstone rises up, the coffin shudders, shaken by internal jolts, splits, and Pierrot springs forth, resuscitated, green with terror.

"Pooh! Phenol!" Lethargy had gripped him, but now fear has cured him. He can breathe, see and hear. What a joy it is to live!

The warden of the cemetery arrives, carrying a lantern in one hand and a bottle in the other. At the sight of Pierrot, he risks falling over, thunderstruck, but Pierrot reassures him, and explains what has happened. The warden holds his sides, deeming the adventure utterly farcical. That vexes Pierrot, but the warden offers him the bottle, and he drinks.

Two sinister heads appear at the top of the white wall and then disappear. A thick mist rises, and fire follets run around.

The warden and Pierrot get drunk. It seems to them that dead souls emerge from the tombs. They see them. Clad in extinct colors, they move through the mist, phantasmal and fugitive, in a fantastic ballet. The music gradually fades away; the sinister heads reappear at the top of the wall, and that intrusion of reality dissipates the fiction; the souls vanish.

The cut-throats, three in number, preceded by their shadows, slide along the wall. They approach treacherously, throw themselves upon the warden, tie him up, gag him, stab him, rob him, climb over the wall again, and disappear.

Pierrot, crouching behind a grave, his eyes wide and his teeth chattering, is a living statue of horror. He contemplates the warden, palpates him, lifts him up, lays him down in his own grave, seals the stone, readjusts the cross and suspends the wreaths from it.

Then he takes a ladder, leans it against the wall, climbs up cautiously and looks over. The coast is clear; he descends on the other side and disappears.

IV

Winter frosts a public square. To the left, the mairie, to the right, the church. A hot chesntut merchant is stoking his brazier.

Pierrot arrives, blowing piteously on his frozen hands. Oh! Chestnuts! He rummages in his empty pockets and asks for credit, which the merchant refuses. Pierrot simulates indifference and disgust. Those chestnuts smell burned, so there! And he goes away, idly looking at the wall of the mairie, where marriage banns are displayed behind iron mesh.

Heavens, what does he see? Columbine is remarrying! That cannot be!

The aged nurse appears, trotting along. She has a yellow shawl and a green bonnet.

"Bonjour," Pierrot says to her. "It's me."

She jumps like a carp, beats the air with her umbrella, tucks up her skirt and runs away.

The priest goes by, in a hurry.

Pierrot salutes him. "*Vade retro, Satanas!*"

The frightened priest exorcizes him and takes refuge in the church.

But here comes the doctor. Pierrot stops him.

"Do you recognize me?"

Oh, what a blunder! But, not wanting to admit it, the physician is annoyed. "Clown, rogue, you're simulating Pierrot, but he's dead—or you're mad. Be careful that I don't have you locked up." He makes off.

Suddenly, a wedding party comes out of the church. The well-dressed Monsieur is giving his arm to Columbine.

Pierrot throws himself upon them. Columbine has an attack of nerves. The Monsieur receives six to nine slaps without flinching, then takes Pierrot's death certificate from his pocket and presents it to him with a superior expression.

"You're dead!"

Pierrot jibs, but the whole wedding party falls upon him, hitting him with canes and umbrellas. Grabbed by two *sergents de ville* he bites the arm of one of them and gouges the eye of the other, but they hold him firmly. And the physician, tearing a leaf out of his notepad, scribbles on it and says:

"He's mad. Take him to Charenton."

V

A courtyard, where madmen are pushing brooms, with no leaves. The gate is open. A concierge is smoking his pipe and looking into the street.

A terrible racket goes up, of howling and barking. A madman races out, followed by the doctor and wardens. He runs through the open gate. Everyone plunges through it behind him. The stage remains empty.

The *sergents de ville* arrive, holding Pierrot. Is there no one to receive him? Weary of waiting, they pin the order to intern Pierrot to the door and tie him to a tree. He is desolate. How can he escape?

Enter Columbine and her second husband. A grave moment; he is showing her the monuments and administrations of the State. Pierrot hides behind the tree,

Charivari and tumult. The captured madman is brought back. The director sponges his face, sacks the warden who has left the gate open and installs a new concierge, then launches himself in pursuit of the madman. Columbine's husband has followed the crowd, idly.

Columbine hears someone calling her.

"Heavens! Pierrot!"

He begs her. She consents to untie him. The concierge is asleep. Pierrot wakes him up. He takes the doctor's paper pinned to the door and holds it out to him.

"Here! Madame and I have brought a madman. He's wandering around somewhere. I recommend him to you."

A hundred-sour coin exchanges hands covertly. Pierrot and Columbine embrace and escape. The well-dressed Monsieur reappears.

"Where's Columbine?"

The concierge examines him: suspect appearance. There's no doubt about it; he's the madman. The director and the wardens are summoned. The well-dressed Monsieur is tied up, given a cold shower and electric shocks, and carried away, three-quarters dead.

In the meantime, Pierrot and Columbine flee toward the blue land of amour and dream.

PIERROT THE NIHILIST

IN PIERROT'S workroom there is a kind of alchemical forge where tints of red fire, stimulated by a gigantic bellows, yawn in crucibles where philtres are boiling. Dusty folios bear such names as Kant, Spinoza and Schopenhauer. A vast blackboard extends, on which these sentences are traced in chalk: *What is God? What is the soul?* followed by enormous question marks.

To the left a gigantic flask rounds out its belly; a furnace is heated from below by the breath of the giant bellows. One also remarks complicated and bizarre scientific apparatus, stuffed lizards, phials of poisons and a death's-head.

Pierrot is alone in a Faustian overcoat. There is the daylight of a winter sky.

Pierrot is alone, meditating the formula written on the blackboard. Wrinkles crease his forehead, contention causes his eyes to bulge from their orbits and his mouth to crease. Oh, to wrench its secret from the unknown! To know the foundation of things, the absolute! Feverishly, he places a formidable equation

under the formula on the blackboard, the X of which
is elusive. Disappointed, he effaces that algebra and
sets about consulting the books of philosophy. He leafs
through them, moistening his finger with saliva; they
do not tell him anything more. Then he dissects one
of the lizards, examines the scales under a microscope,
detaches the tail and sniffs the feet—in vain! He inter-
rogates the death's-head, rummages in its orbits, rubs
its teeth with a corner of his dressing gown, contemplates it, nose to nose, shakes it and, unable to extract
anything from it, throws it into the air. It falls back on
to the neck of a bottle and is impaled there.

Columbine arrives, naked in a corolla of gauze
that inflates and collapses at every step she takes, uncovering the stem of her legs all the way to the pistil,
mysteriously enclosed in a white tutu. She makes reproaches to Pierrot and cajoles him. Oh, the villain, he
is neglecting her for philosophy! She indicates the formula written on the blackbody and makes the horns at
Pierrot. Nonsense! God? The soul? Let it be sufficient
for him to know that she is beautiful; and she puts the
pale pink skin of her arm, and its furry hollow, beneath
his nose. He slaps his forehead . . .

Oh! An idea! Ah, genius—and so simple! Pierrot
goes pale with pride and joy. Kill Columbine, and
thus discover her soul, the soul of beings and things,
which flees under the scalpel and escapes chemical
analysis! With forced, sniggering laughter, he incites
Columbine to enter into the flask. She lends herself to
it, in jest. Immediately, with a diabolical joy, he hangs
on the bellows and stimulates the fire. In a tragic ges-

ticulation induced by asphyxia, Columbine melts and volatilizes in the midst of fireworks.

Pierrot inscribes the result of the incineration on the blackboard: so much hydrocarbon, so much oxygen, so much calcium phosphate, but the soul: zero. He tears his hair in despair. But all is not lost! He has only to kill himself. Being dead, he will know by personal experience. But in order to die it is necessary to commit suicide. How? Swallow a stick of dynamite? Ingurgitate with the aid of the monster bellows a clyster of air that will inflate him until he explodes? Take a sixty-degree bath in vitriol? All of that is repugnant. His only and last resource is to surrender himself to the law and allow himself to be decapitated legally. A gendarme is passing in the street. Pierrot runs to the window and calls to him.

The gendarme appears, moustache turned up all the way to his cockade, legs in a fork and fingers splayed.

Pierrot recounts his crime—the horrible death of Columbine—to the gendarme. The gendarme is horrified; he bristles, shivers, vacillates and faints. Pierrot slaps his hands, makes him respire alkali and, tying his own hands, drags him away, carrying a basket full of test tubes, which he confides forcibly to the policeman.

II

A few weeks later. Pierrot is asleep on a wretched camp bed in the condemned cell. A chamber pot is under the bed, beside the basket containing compasses, magnifying glasses and test tubes.

Enter the judge clad in a toga with a wig on his head: the classic judge of the Guignol. He is holding the sentence in his hand and he wakes Pierrot up, showing him the executioner, hideous in a mask and black coat, who has a wine stain on his face and huge hairy hands, like the feet of a tropical spider. Those enormous hands are brandishing a phenomenal pair of scissors.

"One moment!" says Pierrot to the judge. "I have to talk to you in secret."

He commences by complaining about bugs: the bed is full of them. Then he reasons in this fashion: "Since it's the hour of my death, I want, in accordance with my right and the regulations"—he points to them, pinned to the wall—"to have a good breakfast."

"You have only to command," says the judge, curtly.

Pierror orders succulent things. A café waiter bounds from the wall and serves him on a table erected by magic. Pierrot invites the judge to join him; they stuff themselves with truffled pâtés, poultry as large as calves, and imbibe wines of all colors, singing and dancing to a bacchic chant.

Tipsy, Pierrot taps the judge on the belly and demands a little woman.

"Easy!" says the judge. "There's one close at hand!" And he sketches with an airy gesture the zigzag of a huge figure 8.

"Fie!" says Pierrot "Too delicate."

He sets fire to a cork with the candles of the meal and inscribes in charcoal on the tablecloth the name CLEOPATRA. He demands nothing less.

"Damn!" says the embarrassed judge. He folds himself in two and, under the fist-in-the-guts of inspiration, he summons a hirsute and dishevelled magnetizer, whose nose, forehead and fingers are dripping phosphorus. However, he immediately magnetizes Pierrot. The latter sees Cleopatra spring forth from a trapdoor, in the middle of a rose-bush. She has a tunic slit along the thigh and pearls in her hair. Her smile is divine. She dances lasciviously. Pierrot, rigid, with his eyes closed, appeals to her, drooling with admiration. She disappears.

The judge wakes him, and Pierrot opens his eyes; he sees the executioner in Cleopatra's place. The latter makes the condemned man's toilette, but he (the executioner) has a stomach ache. Pierrot "senses" that and politely offers him his chamber pot.

"Let's go!" says the judge.

A clock chimes cavernously. The door opens. Death is waiting on the threshold, leaning on her scythe. She makes a sign to Pierrot to follow her. He places his hand on his heart, salutes her with a clownish grace, picks up his basket of test tubes, and follows her bravely, preceding the judge and the gendarme.

III

Moonlight is illuminating a corner of a cemetery and a livid wall. In an open coffin next to a freshly-dug grave, Pierrot is lying, decapitated, with his head between his feet.

Sitting on the coffin, Death, scythe in hand is looking at Pierrot. She takes hold of his head by one ear
and lifts it up. She lifts a limp arm, which falls back.
She makes a show of replacing Pierrot's head on his
shoulders, and he immediately sneezes, spits, sniggers
and raises himself up on his elbow. He looks to the left
and the right, and puts his hand to his head as if to
make sure that it will not fall off—a tic that he repeats
periodically.

He finds the coffin narrow and gets to his feet,
pointing at the red line around his neck. He questions
Death; it's an opportunity, if ever there was one, to ask
the difficult ones. He will finally know.

"Who are you?" he asks.

"Death."

"Aha! And God, and the soul, and the world, and
life, and the Devil, and Hell, and time, and space, and
matter?"

Every time, Death shakes her head in a melancholy
fashion.

"What!" cries Pierrot, scandalized. "*Nothing!* There's
nothing, nothing at all; nothing exists?"

Death clicks her thumb on her teeth, expressively.

"Damn!" says Pierrot. "Do you think I'm going to
bury myself in a ditch for *nothing*?"

"It's necessary, though," she says. "Come on." And
she points to the gaping grave.

"Never in this life!"

"I'm taking you."

"No, no, no."

"Oh, you don't know how beautiful I am."

And she starts to dance, exercising upon him the terrible seduction of lust and death. Her shroud tucked up over her fleshless tibias, she smiles and holds out her arms to him. Her bones make a noise like castanets; she dances the tango, and dislocates herself agreeably. Pierrot finds her suave. She attracts him to the edge of the ditch. He tries to seize her, and she extends her lips to him.

Clash of cymbals! He falls into the ditch, and the earth collapses on top of him. A fire follet escapes from the greasy mud.

Death performs a pirouette and pronounces a little compliment, in a line of eight syllables.

PIERROT THE MORMON

To the memory of the Hanlon-Lees.[1]

IN PIERROT'S absence, his three wives are receiving. Little soirée. Black coats and low-cut dresses. Pierrot's father-in-law and mother-in-law are at table with dignity before a tea-urn as stout as a barracks cooking-pot and a pile of sandwiches a meter high.

Pierrot's three golden-haired wives, Za, Cla and Lou,[2] are wearing similar pink dresses; their pale pink

---

1 The Hanlon-Lees were a troupe of acrobats formed in the 1840s by John Lees and the three Hanlon brothers (later joined by their three younger siblings) who performed in many vaudevilles on various Parisian stages, before touring extensively in Europe and America, being recruited by Phineas T. Barnum and being filmed by Thomas Edison; they pioneered the genre of "knockabout comedy" carried forward by the Marx brothers. They were greatly admired by Joris-Karl Huysmans, and their name was preserved long after the present story was written, most notably in the name of the Hanlon-Lees Action Theater founded in the USA in 1979 and still active at rodeos and "Renaissance fairs."

2 It is probably not irrelevant to this nomenclature that one of Catulle Mendès series of stories in the *Écho* humorously detailing the immorality of contemporary Parisian society featured a trio of saucy young women named Jo, Lo and Zo.

complexions are dazzling. They are coming and going, circulating, falling into armchairs, hanging on to the arms of dancers, radiating a gaiety that the absence of their husband renders significant.

Three flirters of preference captivate their attention. Major Bagstock,[1] as fat as a hogshead, oxblood red, with the eyes of a lobster, pleases Za. Cla is smiling at a gentleman planted so stiffly before her that he seems to be taking root in the ground. Lou charms most of all an unstable hunchback, curled up into a ball, with disquieting rubbery shoulders. At that moment a domestic with a tray of glasses bumps into the hunchback, who flies away like a balloon, pirouettes on his axis, collides with the ledge of the cupboard, rebounds on to the fireplace and, rolling with little bounces, returns to nestle against Lou, who does not seem unduly surprised by his disappearance.

Jerky and joyful music. Grave individuals are jigging energetically. An old lady is trampled. A negro in orange livery bounds on to the piano and treads the keys with his feet, like grapes. General enthusiasm, in the midst of which the negro disappears into the piano, the lid of which falls upon him with a bang.

Ladies are gossiping behind their fans. Whist players at a table are playing their cards, so absorbed that their wigs are catching fire on the candle-flames without them noticing. It is pointed out to them, but they continue playing imperturbably, their crania car

---

1 Probably the character featured in Charles Dickens' novel *Dombey and Son* (1846), who pays court to Miss Tox.

bonized, their eyes revulsed in agony and their teeth grinding. Once bald, they extinguish one another.

In the meantime, the gentleman stiffly planted before Cla is stubborn in his deplorable rigidity. He is gradually becoming green, turning into a tree. Imperceptible buds, and then little leaves, are growing at the ends of his arms and on top of his head. In a few minutes, growing visibly in the tropical heat of the chandeliers, it will be permissible to recognize him as a pear tree, of a firm and ligneous substance.

Major Bagstock prepares himself a grog of pure whisky, into which he squashes an egg and a pepper as large as a cucumber. He swallows it hot, without flinching. A little blue flame immediately pearls on his nose. A pragmatic Yankee leaps forward to light his cigar on that beacon. A magisterial punch followed by a catapulting kick precipitates him on to the elastic hunchback, bowling over Mistress Lou, who shows the color of her garters as she is upended. The hunch-back-ball ricochets off the ceiling, flattening a gentle-man like a pancake, and passes through the window of the gallery in a firework display of broken stained glass

In the meantime, very calmly, Pierrot's father-in-law finishes reading the *New York Herald* and his mother-in-law finishes consuming the sandwiches and emptying the tea-urn. As she swallows, she swells; he, on the contrary, gets thinner. When he is no more than a skeleton, she continues swelling, and gradually, detached from the ground, oscillates and flies away through the window.

Universal joy. The father-in-law, liberated from a long slavery, plays a polka on his dental keyboard, with unusual talent. Only one diseased tooth, a false key, produces an intermittent and discordant B flat. The stiff gentleman is already bearing little pears, but they are not yet ripe. As his foliage is too much of a hindrance he is trimmed and pruned painlessly. Then gentlemen and ladies, holding hands, dance an epileptic conga around him.

Pierrot appears on the threshold, to the tune of the *De profundis*. A sad wind blows out the candles. The father-in-law's dental polka expires with a croak. All the lights dim. The dancers become pale—worse than that, livid—as if the white phophorescence of Pierrot's long glabrous face were extending a mortuary reflection over everyone. However, the round-dance continues, silently; at each circuit a link of the chain is detached and the dancer, of whichever sex, salutes Pierrot, who is immobile, like the specter of the Commander,[1] and exits, the women hopping and the men walking on their hands. The last to remain is a short young man whose nose Pierrot seizes; the young man picks his nose. Disgusted, Perrot grabs him with pincers and throws him into the street.

Za, Cla and Lou, meanwhile, surround him, heaping him with caresses, rummaging in his mastic overcoat and the pockets of his dinner-jacket. What gift has he brought them? He does not respond to their cajolery, intrigued by the presence of the arborescent

---

1 In Mozart's opera *Don Giovanni* (1787).

gentleman, from whose elbow he picks a pear, which he peels and eats. It is exquisite. At his gesture, a harvest is made. Then, as the human pear tree is taking up too much room, Pierrot puts his arm around him, embraces him tightly, uproots him with a loud crack of the floorboards, and carries him away, his fibers severed and his roots dangling.

In his absence, Major Bagstock tumbles down the chimney and falls at Za's feet. A balloon squirted through the window knocks over the returning Pierrot and falls flat. It is the rubber hunchback, who is coming back to pay court to Lou. While Cla makes Pierrot respire salts, causing him to sneeze hundred-sou coins, Za and Lou, one pushed by Bagstock and the other by the hunchback, return to their bedrooms to the right and the left, traversing the doors as one might burst through paper hoops.

Pierrot does not show any gratitude for Cla's cares. Installed in his armchair, he invites her to undress, eyeing the sofa lustfully. She refuses, and he does not insist. Smiling, he puts his fingers around her neck and strangles her. She sticks out a tongue like that of a calf, her eyes bulging. He folds her in two and sticks her in a cupboard.

On to another! Before knocking on the door of Lou's bedroom he cocks an ear and looks through the keyhole. Horror! As expected! He resumes his impassivity and adopts a gracious air. Lou appears, in a corset and short skirt. He draws her to him, closes and bolts the door, and commences caressing her. Pretty leg, velvety arm. He points at the sofa. She refuses. He does not insist, and stabs her with his pen-knife. Punctured like a red target, he hides her behind the sofa,

Now for Za! He goes to the door, listens and looks. As expected! He knocks repeatedly, and negotiates through the keyhole. She appears in her chemise. He grabs her, draws her to him and guides her toward the sofa. She resists. He offers her a pastille of prussic acid, that she consents to take, without knowing what it is, without even saying yes, and dies.

Traversing the doors, Major Bagstock and the hunchback spring forth. They have seen everything. Violent reproaches. Briskly, Pierrot evades the blows that the clumsy major aims at him; as for the hunchback, his instability renders him innocuous. He leaps, rebounds, and finishes up smashing the chandeliers. Meanwhile, the phlegmatic Pierrot moves the sofa and opens the cupboard.

At the sight of the three dead women the major faints and the balloon man hides under a sideboard. Pierrot lights a cigar.

Courage and rage return to the major; he swallows a glass of whisky and a raw pepper, and wants to box. Pierrot extends his arms and touches his cigar to the other's lips. The major explodes, the balloon bursts, and the dead women resuscitate with a start. Pierrot smiles; everything collapses.

FEAR

To the mime Séverin[1]

PRUDENTLY, PIERROT pushes the door slowly, so that it appears to be opening on its own. His anxious and fearful plastered face slides behind it, however, and explores.

Is there no one lying in ambush behind the batten? No one.

And Pierrot slips into the room, as flat as a sole, and closes it quickly, so that no one and nothing can come in.

A turn of the key.

Cric-crac.

Let's push the bolt: *click!*

Ha ha!

He rubs his hands, winks, and stands still, like a long ironic moonbeam, in the semi-darkness.

---

1 Séverin Cafferra (1863-1930) was the most significant heir of Deburau in the role of Pierrot, having studied the art of mime under Louis Rouffe, Deburau's own star pupil. He was active and moderately famous when the present story was written.

There! Let's light up.

Groping his way, gripped again by a vague anguish, he bumps into an item of furniture and stumbles, alarmed; shivering, he heads for the fireplace. Spectrally, he recoils, his finger pointing to an intruder: his pale twin, a vague reflection in the mirror. Imbecile! Afraid of his own image!

He lights two candles, and sees himself more clearly.

Yes, it's me . . . me? Me!

Strangeness and mystery.

Me! Myself . . . ? Me! My hands, my body, my face. my mouth, my eyes. Very pale, very thin, mortuary face, the holes of the orbits, the laughing teeth, rigid, immobile, dead. *Brr!*

He looks at the candles. They are vacillating bizarrely. Why? A breath passes. Where is it coming from? With his mouth, he imitates the mystery of the wind skimming the ground, weeping under doors, entering, invisible but alive. A being, a presence: it is there. And the flames vacillate, disquieting.

Oh yes, disquieting. What an unusual and unexpected aspect the rooms in which one lives can take on! What is hiding under the veil of the coat-stand? Nothing. Over there, that form hanging in the shadowed covert, what is it? Oh, what is it? One might think it a cadaver!

Let's arm ourselves with the fire-tongs . . . no, rather with this cudgel. What if it's a ruse, some thief or assassin lying in wait? Let's strike!

The garment falls, an empty rag.

Undoubtedly, it's nothing, but who knows whether someone behind the door might be spying on me, waiting for me to go to sleep in order to break the lock and . . . *Shh! Shh!* Let's approach on tiptoe . . . ear to the wood, closely applied . . . Yes, yes, there's someone there, behind the door. If I were to open it, oh, two hooked hands would seize me by the throat. Someone's breathing, yes, someone's breathing behind the door . . .

No, it's me, it's my own breath, it's my own heart that I can hear.

He returns to the middle of the room, moving slowly, his index finger in his eye and his smile crooked.

A gaze is peering through the keyhole, and one suddenly senses oneself transpierced by an inexplicable anguish. It's the gaze that has struck you, treacherously. Let's block it up! Lock it! Don't let the malefactor in!

With a flat, trembling hand, and then with a screwed-up piece of paper introduced into the keyhole, Pierrot blocks the gap, as one might put out an eye.

Is that enough? No, a barricade! That chest of drawers, that table, the chair! Good. But there's still the window. Someone is applying a ladder to the sill. Rung by rung, barefoot, he's climbing. He's climbing! His face appears in the pane; his fist staves it in; the catch yields. He launches himself . . .

On the knees. *Don't kill me. Mercy! Pity!*

Eyes wide with horror, mouth agape, Pierrot stands up again.

Because there's nothing there, no one . . . No one but me, and my frisson. No matter; let's make sure that the window is firmly closed. Let's close the curtains. Seeing nothing is reassuring.

As soon as said, it's done. He notices that the plate of the chimney is raised.

I don't like that. Someone might come down through the flue, tumbling like a ball—he imitates that—like a big fat spider gathered on the floor; then the figure extends again; the arms grow, the head swells, the legs elongate—he increases immeasurably—and then he . . .

Pierrot perceives himself, terrifying, in the mirror.

Oh, that's how he'll be, haggard and horrible, what an image! Let's hide that image! I don't want to see it any more. I don't want to see myself! I frighten myself!

He snatches the curtains from the bed, veils the mirror and slowly wipes away the sweat from his moist forehead.

What's that noise? Zzz! Zzz! A strange vibration! Ah, that big fly; it's repulsive; it isn't a fly like any other! How it drones! Zzz! Zzz!

He gives chase to it; with the cunning of an Apache, he catches it eventually; it escapes; he lashes out with a duster, and with a great horrified gesture, arms raised, foot retracted, scraping the floor, he crushes it.

A great silence, a long malaise.

That smell? Is that a smell? Yes, something has the odor of death, of ruination. Is it that cupboard? (*He sniffs it.*) Is it my hands? No. Those flowers, then, the flowers in that vase! That's it, those dead flowers in stagnant water. Throw them away; it's quite simple. But it would be necessary to open the door . . .

He doesn't dare.

Open the window?

He doesn't dare.

Throw them in the fireplace and raise the plate?

He doesn't dare,

Well, let's go to sleep. Sleep calms, reposes. One can't. Yes, yes! One thinks, one dreams, one starts, one shivers, one has the nightmare crouching on one's breast. No matter! There are mild, angelic slumbers, child-like slumbers. Let's try to sleep.

He approaches the bed.

Oho! What suspicion! Very small already, then big, then a man, that apprehension: at the moment when, one knee on the bed, one lifts the other foot off the floor, to feel a hand, oh, a hand, emerge from under the bed, which seizes the foot, oh, and pulls it. Madness! There's no one under the bed. There's never anyone under the bed. Besides which, one can look, with the candle. For greater prudence, let's arm ourselves!

He takes a knife from the kitchen, tries the point on his finger, the edge on the sole of his shoe. A good knife!

Let's go!

On his knees, face down, he screws up his eyes, waves his arm under the bed, moves the light around, searches with the knife.

I knew it; there's no one there. Let's go to bed.

He puts his knee on the bed, but can't decide to lift his foot off the floor.

Hup!

He doesn't dare.

What are you afraid of? *Hup!*

He doesn't dare.

Let's count to three. One, two . . .

He can't decide to say *three.*

Come on, it's stupid, shrug the shoulders!

Three! Let's go!

The foot rises; an invisible hand catches it, maintains it, and, in the imaginary grip, shaking the leg imprisoned by terror, Pierrot turns round, his face petrified, the mask of the petty death; he kicks desperately, snatches himself away from the hallucinatory hand, and, with the convulsive tremor of a hunted beast, takes refuge in a corner of the room, huddles there with a spasm and a hoarse sob and curls up, pulling in his limbs and head like a tortoise.

These panics are truly intolerable. What means is there of escaping them? Oh, one means!

And his hands implore celestial clemency.

Sleep . . . he knows full well that he won't sleep. Escape . . . escape from himself, at any price. Drunkenness, then?

To open a cupboard with a mad gesture, to break the neck of a bottle on the table and drink, drink in one gulp, that's it, that's it! Yes, that's better. He can breathe! He shakes pleats of gripping anguish from his ample garment. He banishes hostile appearances. He expels baleful forms. He sniggers; he triumphs; he spits on fear.

But *he*, or *she*, is there.

Someone spoke!

Pierrot's lips move.

He has heard!

A breath has passed.

Mystery!

Someone has come in, on tiptoe.

He walks, he looks, he passes by!

It's the specter of Fear, of livid Fear, with mad eyes, with shivering arms and knocking knees.

Ah! Ah! It's there! It's standing up, it's opening its arms, it's grabbing me!

Pierrot utters a hysterical, heart-rending scream; the *aura* passes over him like a storm wind. He beats the air with his white wings and falls, struck down by the invisible.

DREAMS AND HAUNTINGS

THE REVENANT

MADAME HASTIER was chaste and devout. So the first thing she did, on returning from the funeral, when her friends had bid her goodbye definitively, was to retire to her room and kneel down on a prie-Dieu. She elevated her soul in prayer, trying to forget all the wrongs that her husband had inflicted on her, the cruelty of the years they had lived together in a complete mental and physical divorce, the bitterness of the money squandered by Hastier, his orgies with prostitutes, his insolence and brutality toward her: a thousand insults that she had drunk to the lees, initially by virtue of Christian humility and then because, being penniless, she was at the mercy of that man.

It was over, then; he was dead, quite dead; a cerebral congestion had struck him down after a night of pleasure and drunkenness. He had just been carried away, nailed between four fir-wood planks, on a bed of wood-shavings. She would never see him again, with his heavy hog-like body—a resemblance, accentuated by a long snout, to some obscene animal with an evil malice in its little hooded eyes. Hastier would not make her suffer any more. She would never again see him come back at seven o'clock in the morning, his white cravat ragged, his shirt-front dirty and crumpled, his face troubled and his eyes bloodshot. The beast was dead. And, stiff, deformed and hideous, it was reposing in a hole under the ground!

"My God," sighed Madame Hastier, "may your will be done. May your holy name be blessed."

Her mother came in at that point: a very old woman with sharp pale blue eyes and a thin and cynical mouth.

"Good riddance my poor child," she said, unceremoniously. And she gazed, with a half-smile, at the empty room, in which a mortuary disarray remained; she shook her head as she contemplated her daughter, tall and thin in her full mourning-dress, her complexion dry and slightly acned, as abstinence does to devotees. She seemed to be saying: "We're finally going to respire, to take life easy!"

But an imperceptible tremor was agitating the old woman's nostrils; a malaise lifted her upper body in an involuntary shrug. In spite of the open windows and the autumnal chill already in the air, the terrible odor of death was perceptible, an imprecise heavy stink that did not resemble anything else, a greasy and pharmaceutical sweat, profoundly acrid,

Madame Hastier turned her eyes away, out of modesty. She saw her husband again in his final costume, an enormous mass flattened in the sheets under the flowers; the head seemed to be drawn in, hiding in the pillows; all the could be seen was the bald cranium and

a black chin-strap; the hands—crossed, of course—
were terrible, swollen and knotty, of a livid white in
which green veins snaked. A weight of a thousand ki-
los seemed to be weighing upon the body, so absolute
and terrible did its rigidity seem.

And to think that *that* had once been loved, that
she had loved it, that they had been together, heart to
heart and flesh to flesh, for years! Then she thought
about her long celibacy since, her claustral virginity
within the marital state, like the Christians of the first
age who lived chastely beside their spouses. And because her nerves were exhausted, she wept.

✳

At dinner, she and her mother could not eat. They
took a little broth, but the meat was taken away without their having touched it; an invincible repugnance
followed them in all the petty actions of their habitual
life; it seemed to them that a tenacious and suspect fluid
was bathing them. Since the morning they had been
washing their hands continually, with the sensation that
something greasy always remained on their fingers. And
they had the horror of sensing that they too were made
of flesh, of perishable and corruptible mud.

They only drank tea, unable to support the odor
of wine.

Then they went to bed early.

As soon as she was in bed, Madame Hastier's en-
ervation increased. Through the door, left open, she
could hear her mother's respiration in the next room.:

an old, petty, dry respiration traversed by asthmatic whistling, as if a candle were being blown out at a distance. That ought to have reassured her. On the contrary, she had a desire to wake the sleeper; if she did not do it, it was out of respect for her age, and in order not to appear to be afraid. But, not being able to sleep, she got up, her head on fire, her body agitated by fever. She was searching on her work-table for *The Imitation of Christ* when, suddenly very pale, she looked at the curtains. Then, candle in hand, she opened them abruptly. A little creak escaped from the mirror-fronted wardrobe. Madame Hastier could feel her heart beating; she stayed there momentarily, motionless, listening to the seconds palpitate to the tick-tock of the clock. Suddenly, shivering, she couched down and looked under the bed.

She remained on her knees, in her chemise, repeating her prayers. But her nerves, in her body, which was free and naked under the linen, perceived the unspeakable contact of fear, the invisible presence that horripilates the flesh and makes the hair stand on end. She had never thought about Hastier as she did this evening; she saw him again—a strange obsession—young, as in the first days of their honeymoon period; she recalled his caresses, things that had troubled her strangely then, although she had been dead subsequently to almost all carnal sensation.

She remembered singular cases of conscience, doubts that she had suffered after conjugal night, and reported to her confessor, permissions that she had been obliged on his orders to refuse to her husband.

Why was she thinking about that now? Hastier was gone, disappeared forever from the empty house; why was she feeling the haunting of his lustful person like this?

Perhaps it was a suggestion of the Evil One? She made a large sign of the cross, and before going back to bed, she sprinkled her sheets with holy water.

She was sleeping profoundly when it seemed to her that her bed fled beneath her, like the floor of a descending elevator. She also had the sensation of a boat sinking and gliding on the surface of water. She ceased to perceive the weight of her covers and the warmth of the bed. A sensation of cold invaded her as if she had been uncovered, and at the same time, it seemed to her that her body was free, and naked to the air; she could not even feel the light friction of her chemise any longer.

All that was so rapid, and happened in a slumber so profound, in which she remained tied down, passive and devoid of strength, that she could not react and wake up, in spite of her will, even though, within her troubled dream, a slight, inexplicable sensation of sensuality enveloped her, perhaps nothing other than the coolness of her flesh, freed on any veil. But immediately, she felt that she was touched, palpated and caressed. It was gentle and singular, and she would have abandoned herself to the irrational pleasure if the fear of diabolical suggestions had not persisted in her sleep.

She extended her arms, and made an effort to wake up, but in vain; and the fluid contact suddenly became more precise. She felt invested by something soft and warm, which resembled flesh plunging into her own, but which nevertheless remained as imponderable and as subtle as air. The impression of a body inflated by wind, of a human balloon embracing her with soft and sticky caresses, was what she experienced, something simultaneously bizarre and sweet, which was now making her swoon, defenselessly, savoring a mysterious—she was conscious of it—exquisite and infamous joy.

Then she felt herself taken entirely; invisible lips stuck to hers, sucker-like, and by virtue of everything certain, untranslatable and special that betrays and denounces the existence of a familiar being, she divined and understood that it was the dead man who had returned, having escaped, sly and bestial, through the pores of the coffin and the clods of greasy earth, who had flown away in his astral form and had realized, after so many years of mutual divorce, the crime of satisfying himself upon her and violating her! What she felt was delightful and horrible, a charm of ancient and distant caresses alternated with disgust for the debauchery of recent years. She believed herself to be damned for that sin, involuntary and yet permitted, almost with her consent. A vague pious supplication persisted within her throughout the nightmare and the torture, and she repeated strangely: "Oh, Jesus, Marie, help me!" while her lips smiled lasciviously.

And her sensuality suddenly became so painful, and so atrocious, that she awoke.

✳

It was daylight. She observed with stupor that she was as naked as on the day of her birth. The mortuary odor, although attenuated, was still floating. The bed was unmade, turned upside down.

Madame Hastier, cruelly confused and red, dressed in haste; she felt soiled. She went to take a bath and thus purify herself. Then she went into a church, although it was very early, and confessed to the first priest who was willing to hear her.

He remained silent momentarily, and then coughed lightly in the shadow of the confessional, behind the grille, and said in a blank and atonal voice: "The ways of the demon are obscure. Sin is always there, lying in wait for us. Pray, Madame, and repeat every evening, before you go to bed, the litanies of the Most Holy Virgin."

SENSATIONS OF ETHER

GEORGES raised his eyes from his book. Under the table, the sound of mice, the faint rustle of papers, continued. He leaned over and murmured softly: "Darling!"

Lost in her occupation, aureoled by a circle of yellow light, a pale little girl, without hearing him, was cutting out embryonic forms of animals and people with her father's large scissors. Her long silky blonde hair framed her slender, pensive face, absorbed and distant.

"Little darling," he repeated.

She shuddered, extracted from her ecstatic work, and raised pale blue eyes upon him, vague and bright. A melancholy smile finally brushed her mouth; a warm flash of tenderness was exhaled by her features.

Already reclaimed by her childish task—a bird with a large beak and a long tail that she was cutting out— she had departed again, her mind elsewhere.

"My God," he murmured, dolorously, "how she resembles her mother!"

A vice squeezed his heart, it was struck like an anvil by repeated and redoubled hammer-blows, and then pincers twisted and shook that sick heart as if to tear it out. The frightful oppression, the sharp pain—probably symptoms announcing angina, the physician thought—suffocated him with a clutching anguish.

Oh, no, don't think about it, don't think any more!

And since the sight of the child made him feel ill, he reached out for the bell—but at the idea that Claudine, taken away by the maidservant, might cry, his courage failed.

Poor little thing, it's not her fault!

And again the obsession gripped him, in the throes of physical and mental torture.

How she resembles her mother!

Her mother, a bigger Claudine, but not much bigger, a birdlike being, a child, a delightfully pretty white body, a face of a blonde fay with sky blue eyes, like those little pools of water, those doll-sized lakes in which the azure is reflected after rain! Her mother, a chimerical creature of dream, poor little crackbrain! Now so far away, so far, departed in a tragic gust of wind, taken away in a storm of passion by a lover, leaving behind a husband who loved her and the other Claudine, who reminded him of her so cruelly, her daughter, the little blonde girl with the paper birds!

Six months already! What was the point of pursuing her? A lawsuit? Drag through the mud a name so dear, still and nevertheless dear? Would a divorce separate them any more? Strike, then, kill the lover, the treacherous friend who had dishonored friendship and stolen his wife? Alas, why do him harm, and her, if she were happy with that man, if she preferred him? Would bloodshed satisfy the frightful jealousy of the husband? By virtue of modesty, tenacious amour, pity and a torturing delicacy, he had sacrificed everything: his anger, his worldly honor, and his thirst for vengeance. As long as she was happy, the culpable. ingrate Claudine, the spoiled child, irresponsible, alas . . .

He might die of it, but what did it matter?

Oh, he would certainly die of it one day, a day of atrocious suffering, when he has stirred the idea too violently in his heart, as one turns over a log in a red-hot fire. Mechanically, with a gesture of touching the wound, in order to escape that torture, for a moment at least, he took a bottle of ether from a casket and, prostrate on the divan, in the shadow, he inhaled the acrid odor recklessly.

A cowardice? Yes, undoubtedly, if that is what it is to want to evade pain and demand from the remedy more than relief: a repose, an alleviation, almost a pleasure. That pleasure, although negative and all forgetfulness, Georges had been seeking for several weeks, without deluding himself regarding the peril. But was not the essential thing not to think any longer, not to feel any longer, not to exist any longer? On certain days, too rare, ether provided that.[1]

---

1 When this story was published, Jean Lorrain, Margueritte's colleague in the *Écho* stable and fellow habitué of the *grenier* had not yet begun publishing his "tales of an ether-drinker" in the *Écho*, but he made no secret of the hallucinations he had suffered when drinking ether in order to stay awake and meet his deadlines for his regular contributions to newspapers.

With the neck of the little bottle introduced hermetically into his nostrils, he experienced, as on the other occasions, at the first exhalations of the evaporating liquid, a relaxing wellbeing, a confused heaviness of the head; his eyelids closed, a softness overtook him, and he entered into the limbo where slumber goes to float. But a dolor ran over his thin face, an electric fulguration, a black spark in his abruptly reopened eyes, in the depths of their ringed cavities.

"Claudine!" he appealed.

Recalled by the pain to consciousness of his paternal obligations, he added: "You'll catch cold; go sit in the armchair next to the fire, darling."

The child obeyed, huddling before the burning logs in the large armchair with the straight sculpted back. Georges watched her, thoughtfully, as she contemplated the embers, and a bitter smile tugged at his lips. In her pose, her elbow folded on the arm of the chair and sustaining the tilted head, the child resuscitated, mysteriously, her mother. How many times had Claudine, absent-mindedly, sat like that, motionless, dreaming of . . . what? Amour? The lover?

Violently, Georges inhaled the ether, in slow and powerful sniffs, drinking the fluid with full nostrils. The charm operated more forcefully. The heaviness of the head was accentuated, a slight buzzing in the ears surrounded him with the muted sound of a crowd, of a circulation of people; he thought he was in populous streets, on the boulevard, with Claudine, always; but that crowd was walking in the swarming silence of a population of shadows; the noise that it was making,

Georges divined, but did not hear. For a second time, he opened his eyes, and saw that he was alone, in his study, with his daughter. There, the excessively true nightmare resumed, obsessively. He wanted to flee the adultery, his pain, his solitude, and abolish himself in the bottle, his eyes closed.

Now he was wandering in a shipyard where a hundred thousand hammers were striking sonorous iron girders, rivets were being placed and holes bored: a deafening racket, with intense vibrations, pounded his skull, striking his temples with a brutal and strident rhythm. That accelerated; the hammers made the air resound for ten leagues around; the wind of their curved trajectories was sensible, and the windows of the apartment trembled.

Georges reopened his eyes and everything disappeared. He plunged back into the mirage.

Every aspiration now lifted him above the divan, without resistance, as light as a feather, toward the ceiling; but each expiration brought him down, heavier than lead and plunged him into the floor. Every time, he rose up higher and fell deeper; from one second to the next his lightness increased, in direct proportion to his weight. He went up in a balloon, cleaving through the azure constellated with stars; the moon inundated him with its milky mildness and he drank its warm radiance; an extraordinary lightness exalted him, and he felt himself still rising, floating higher, ever higher. But when, out of breath, it was necessary for him to descend again, there was the vertigo, slow at first and then accelerated, of a fall. He fell, and fell, losing consciousness, and awoke on the ground, flattened and broken, all his limbs bent. Then he rose up again, and the infinity of those divine or horrifying sensations only lasted a quarter of a second for him.

Then time and space took on enormous proportions and his soul, deformed into a prism, no longer appeared to be his own. He lived other lives, inhaling the essence and exhaling it until he fainted. But a vague notion of identity, a thread that he could not break, always recalled him to existence and forced him, in spite of his resistance, to open his eyes, to recapture, like a drunken man, possession of his self, of his frame, of his thought, of his being. That rupture of the mirage, that disappearance of the magic, that knowledge of the immanent reality of things and of himself were, for him, the most atrocious of awakenings. Fortunately, a residue of intoxication quickly submerged his thoughts, maintaining him semi-dazed, numbed, almost oblivious—very vague, at any rate.

This time, he had a surprise, a joy. Although he had just opened his eyes, his ecstasy still persisted, The study, the lamp, the fire and little Claudine, still motionless in the armchair, conserved an unreal existence, a dream magicality, a hallucinatory reflection. They continued the mirage, and Georges saw that a lateral movement was carrying the room and the divan on which he was lying from right to left. The lampshade was rotating on its own. Then there was a vertical upward and downward movement, and a sudden magnification of things; like elastic being stretched, they were elongated, endowed with life. And little Claudine appeared as a woman. No, she was no longer Claudine the dainty dreamer of the paper birds, but big Claudine, the Claudine who had followed a lover, the unnatural mother, the adulterous wife—but so childlike, alas! In any case, was she not there, returned? But then, did all that truly exist? No, of course not. Georges had had a strange nightmare. But his Claudine, his lunatic little wife with eyes of blue lake had never left him. And the proof . . . !

He murmured: "Claudine!"

And she raised her eyes upon him.

He stammered: "You love me, don't you?"

She nodded her head affirmatively.

"Come and kiss me."

The door opened; the maidservant announced dinner; then, before the haggard silence of the dreamer, Claudine came to tug his silence, appealing: "Papa! Papa!"

Georges made a somersault so abrupt that the bottle of ether fell and broke. Immediately, everything shrank in his eyes; the study became very small; Claudine became a dwarf again, the wife and young mother transformed into a pale, thin girl, who was looking at him fearfully, repeating with the same timbre of voice as the disappeared woman: "Come on then, Papa, come on . . ."

Frightfully pale, he examined the child, and then the maidservant, passing a hand over his brow once or twice, while he compressed his sick heart with the other. Oh, so sick!

Then, getting to his feet, tottering on flaccid legs, he murmured, effortfully: "Yes, darling, let's go to dinner."

THE PIERCED CHAIR

MONSIEUR JUETTE, curé of Boulaine-en-Brie, was an eccentric. He went to say mass at Poussage, a village neighboring Boulaine, on a velocipede, and he had no incumbent. It was even claimed that he brought the viaticum to the dying in a little box attached to the front of his bicycle, and that the warning bell then replaced the choirboy's hand-bell. It was publicly notorious that, having been provoked and challenged to a race to the first house in Boulaine by a band of velocipedists in a merry mood, he had won the improvised match by six lengths, and had received an ovation. He was, furthermore, an excellent fellow, slightly bad-tempered and something of a "crackpot," according to old Huruge, his housekeeper, but "worthy," tall and jovial, as simple and pure as good bread.

However, he was overfond of bric-à-brac and old furniture. Collecting was his mania and all the second-hand dealers in the region knew him. His house was full of old sideboards, Louis XV wooden armchairs, pewter jugs, and cast iron firedogs—a "heap of rubbish," so Huruge said. He had no peer for going into a peasant's cottage, immediately spotting an old and rare object, and being able, via cunning detours full of finesse, to buy it at a low price. His pleasure, as with all true collectors, was in inverse ratio to the dearness of the acquisition; but he was not avaricious, and when he paid ten sous for something worth ten francs, the poor always profited from the good bargain to the extent of at least half the difference.

One evening, he returned late for dinner, to the great discontentment of the housekeeper, who considered any attempt at independence as a personal insult. He was accompanied by a peasant who was carrying an old cane chair, the bottom of which formed a box while the back and legs, finely molded, were ornamented with bouquets of flowers sculpted in the wood.

"Put it there, my good man," he said to the peasant, and as the table was laid, he poured him a large glass of wine and held it out to him, a liberality that Huruge contemplated with indignation. As soon as the man had left, Monsieur Juette rubbed his hands, and caressed the chair amorously.

"Isn't it pretty, and delicate? Come on, Huruge, can you feel the beauty of the piece? Admire the exquisite curve of the feet, the camber of those contours! Do you know what I paid for it? Fifteen sous, my good woman, fifteen sous—and it's worth fifty francs! It's not even damaged; there isn't a centime's-worth of repair-work to be done. And it's the purest Louis XV."

Huruge, tight-lipped but intimidated by the real value of the object, ausculted it, tapping it suspiciously. The cane seat, which she shook lightly, suddenly sprang up in her hand, uncovering the depths of the box and an opening as round as a full moon, for sitting on.

"Oh!" she said, scandalized. "But it's a pierced chair!"

"What did you think it was?" riposted the curé, with a good-humored laugh.

"Well!" she exclaimed. "Well!" And in the kitchen, to which he had retired, Monsieur Juette heard her muttering: "He'll be accumulating chamber pots next! What a mania! Must he have such ideas?"

All through dinner the curé only had eyes for the little pierced chair, truly exquisite and so delicate in its naively cynical significance that there was no suggestion of indecency or obscenity, but something touching, like a corporeal weakness of a woman or child, perfectly natural, in sum, in the needs of our poor humanity. It was not one of those gross and inconvenient pieces of furniture that respond to masculine comfort but a small, discreet item that retained grace and charm in its obscure role and which one could imagine in the past, located in the wardrobe of some elegant marquise, hidden behind a screen, the uncovered full-moon eye of which had only ever seen the white and delicate roundnesses of a plump grand dame or a soubrette—at the most, of a petty abbé surprised by some indisposition, and never, but never, the massive and ignoble rumps of fat seigneurs or financiers. That poor little chair, enslaved to humiliating functions but which nevertheless had nothing vulgar about it, retained in the smile of its sculpted bouquets and the slimness of its body the mischievous grace of a page and a little of the artistic beauty that divinizes everything.

Monsieur le Curé had frequent distractions during his dessert. He could not conceive the stupidity of peasants, and the fact that he had been able to make such a find. He praised the Lord with a grateful heart, and read his breviary devotedly before going up to bed. Once in bed, it took him some time to go to sleep. The little chair was on his mind, and he had difficulty restraining himself from getting up and going downstairs, candle in hand, in order to contemplate it again. The fear that Huruge might hear him retained him; and, in any case, such thoughts, and such an attachment to a terrestrial object, however bizarre or precious it might be, were only vanities.

Gradually, he drifted off to sleep, but only to produce agitated and incoherent dreams, fulgurant images and flashes of sensation—all the confusion and collision of a nightmare, of which the little pierced chair was the soul and the focal point, with radiations in all directions that began or ended there. Always, Monsieur le Curé found it, a mute actor, in all the zigzags and intersections of the unconscious cerebral drama that he was living.

The absurd logic of dreams! By way of a thread broken and renewed a hundred times over, a confused and bizarre action, with multiple twists and turns, unfurled in the *camera obscura* of his brain. An exquisite face with scintillating eyes with a rosy smile appeared to him, a head sprinkled with powder, with a beauty spot in the corner of the eye and another in the corner of the mouth: the most delectable face of a Louis XV marquise that one could see.

He could not doubt that it was La Pompadour;[1] although he had never seen her he recognized her; her cleavage was bare, with a necklace of pearls on a black velvet ribbon around the neck. A voluminous dress of pale blue silk with bouquets of roses made the most of her charming figure. And there was, without him knowing how, an intimate rapport between her and the chair confected for her usage, and which, suddenly transformed by the magic of the dream, became a pierced chair of rosewood and lemonwood, with incrustations of lacquer and silver. If the lid were lifted, a mirror framed with bouquets of roses suggested in advance the reflection of the prettiest rotundities in the world, and the intimate vase, instead of porcelain, was made of gold.

By virtue of a few ludicrous transitions and detours, the décor vanished; the wardrobe in which the marquise had appeared momentarily, with the face of a pretty chambermaid behind her, gave way to subterrains in which Monsieur Juette, pursued by a nameless terror, was fleeing, with his hair standing on end and sweat on his brow, carrying in his arms, like a child being rescued, the pierced chair, in which, he knew, Madame de Pompadour's jewels had been hidden.

Why did he emerge, breathlessly, into an immense square where thousands of heads were swarming in a

---

1 Jeane-Antoinette Poisson, Marquise de Pompadour (1721-1764) was Louis XV's most famous "official mistress." She also established a reputation as a patroness of the *philosophes*, lending important support to Voltaire.

frightful dusk, while a phrase: *The Terror! The Terror!* sounded a sad and icy knell within him? How was it that men in carmagnoles armed with pikes were snatching away the chair that he was still cradling in his arms, and why did he recognize it, immeasurably magnified, hoisted on to a platform, so bizarrely disposed that its interior lid, lifted into the air with its empty disk, outlined against a steel-blue sky the lunette of a guillotine?

The guillotine! The guillotine! It was obvious, and so simple; how had he not realized it sooner? And a voice, as dull and vague as the sea, the whisper of that people with a thousand heads, murmured very softly: "Royalty is about to be decapitated!" Standing on an infamous cart, with her arms bound, Madame de Pompadour arrived, shaken by jolts like the pitching of a boat, above those heads accumulated like waves. But, while still being the marquise, it was no longer the delicate face and fine powdered head of a little while ago; the slender body in a pale blue dress sewn with flowers had given way to a massive virago with a bestial white muzzle and the smile of a prostitute.

She climbed, without aid, the steps of the scaffold to the height of the strange instrument; she readied herself, before all the people, tucking up her shirts with a gesture and passing into the round lunette of the guillotine-chair not her head but her rump, the orb of which fulgurated for an instant, and then was no more, abruptly dispatched to the heavens, in which the moon itself was floating over the presently-empty square, deserted and silent, where only Abbé Juette was weeping, sitting on the little chair, which had reverted to its original form, extending his hands despairingly toward that obscene and ironic moon, which filled the starless night with its golden light.

A shrill snigger rippled, a cloud veiled the moon, and in a whiff of sulfur and a great red light, Satan appeared, with the body of a goat, struck the ground with his hoof and disappeared, in just the time required to exist and to vanish.

Monsieur le Curé jumped so forcefully that he woke up.

It was daylight. Utterly ashamed, he made the sign of the cross several times, plunged in his washbasin, and shook off the frightful impurity of his vision with a prolonged snort. Then he started to pray before going to say the first mass.

When he returned, without even sparing a glance for the little pierced chair, innocent cause or not, but cunning in sin, he sent it away with a deep sigh of regret, carried by Huruge as a gift to the hospice for the poor of the commune.

THE ENCHANTED GARDEN

To Paul Rougier[1]

I

"DON'T you think," de Vins said to me, extending toward the flames his long, pale and slender, effeminate hands, so cold that the heat reddened them without warming them, "that the places in which one lives become impregnated with a particular atmosphere, of a soul floating in invisible particles and mysterious effluvia? That explains the malaise that nervous individuals like us sense in the emptiness of certain rooms, as we feel it in the presence of their owners, surely strangers, hostile members of another race with nothing in common with us?"

He directed eyes at me of a singular blue, bright

---

1 Probably the lawyer, political economist and journalist Jean-Claude-Paul Rougier (1826-1901), who signed many of his writings "Paul Rougier," although the name is not uncommon and was passed on to both his son and grandson, the latter becoming a notable philosopher usually known as Louis Rougier.

and intense: a strange faience blue that still retained the brightness of the firing.

"Isn't the best proof," he continued," that one sleeps badly in hotel rooms? That isn't, I believe, a vain fear of thieves, but because too many lives have passed that way, lain in that bed, worn out the carpet and the napkins. A waistcoat button or a hairpin found in the drawer of the night table gives you the sensation of a veritable intruder, the idea that you have mistaken the room and that someone is about to reenter it."

His tall, slender silhouette was outlined on the gray daylight of the window, thinned by the mourning of his black garments; he had worn no others since Madame de Vins had died three years before.

He went on: "During the winter stations that my wife's illness imposed on us, sometimes in Nice, sometimes in Algiers, once in Palermo and another time in Cannes, I never felt the influence of the milieu more keenly than in those villas whose banal luxury imitates the richest décor and which, hired out every season to cosmopolitan convalescents, and sometimes also to death-throes, by virtue of the disposition of their Italian-style terraces and their large windows open to the sun, resemble sanitaria for exotic clients. I remember one villa above all, with a garden that was positively enchanted, the troubling air of which, charged with fluid languor, was unhealthy for us to respire, like the fever of a stagnant pond or the malaria of certain shadowed places. A maleficent influence weighed upon us there and bewitched our hearts; I only discovered later where it came from."

De Vins contemplated the flames momentarily, and went on:

"We had come to spend that winter in Cannes. Of all the villas signaled to us by the proprietor of the hotel where we were staying, and all those the estate agent enabled us to explore, none suited us. We were wondering whether we ought not to take our winter journey further, to San Remo or Naples, when, in the course of an excursion by automobile, we passed a large garden bordered with walls, at the back of which, masked by treetops, stood an old house with ivy-clad walls. It bore a sign: To LET. I rang at the gate, whose bars were protected by sheet metal that prevented the interior of the garden from being seen.

"An old lame gardener came to open up to us. What is the source of sudden sympathies and antipathies? Scarcely had I glimpsed him than he displeased me. He had a surly expression, annoyed at being disturbed. He preceded us, however, ready to enable us to visit the house. Around us, meanwhile, an enchantment floated, a sense of wonder. There were no other flowers there than roses, which grew tumultuously, flourishing deliriously, entangled in cascades, climbing up the trees, throwing bridges of creepers from one to another.

"A primitive and charming artistry seemed to have organized that disorder, in which a harmony was detectable. Here there was a virgin forest, a folly of ardent bushes of pale golden roses that were as flamboyant as church candles in the sunlight; there, pathways snaked, cut out with shears, in which all the roses, crimson and white, at the same height, traced something like the borders of Indian carpets. Further away, large pools of black water extended, around which were large garnet roses; elsewhere, an entire portico of moss roses resembled a temporary altar of the Fête-Dieu. A gust of wind caused excessively open roses to shed petals like snowflakes; nascent buds seemed to be opening visibly, alive. The complex, multiodorous and yet unique perfume that the garden exhaled was extraordinary; it was intoxicating and soporific, appeasing and mollifying; the soul swooned there; an infinite soft melancholy moistened the eyelids; one did not desire anything, one did not suffer, and one had something akin to a desire to die. I shall never forget with what exotic eyes my wife turned toward me and the suppliant tone in which she murmured to me: 'Oh! Roger . . . !'

"That plea was more than an order for me; so, when we had visited the house, furnished not with the strict and full luxury that we had seen in other villas, the banality of which wearied us, but with fine and true furniture. almost all old, upholstered in rich old-fashioned fabrics that gave a noble and rare physiognomy, like a sad elite soul, to the dwelling, perhaps a little too damp but which a fire maintained day and night would dry out; once we had taken our leave of the gardener, we immediately headed for the house of the advocate to whom with was necessary to address ourselves in order to rent La Rosaire, as the villa of roses was called.

"The businessman received us immediately, with cold, dry politeness and the curt and sober gestures that his peers often have. When he read the terms of the lease to us he declared:

"'I must warn you of one formal and *sine qua non* condition, the rigor of which might perhaps alarm madame; a stipulation the obligation of which cannot be avoided on any pretext by the tenants, to respect the garden in its smallest detail, and not to turn to their profit *any* of the roses that grow there freely. To pick a single one of those roses would be contrary to the testamentary will of the defunct proprietor and would expose you to an annulment of the lease and demands for compensatory damages on the part of the present heir, who only entered into possession of La Rosaire on condition of respecting herself the desires of the defunct lady, her mother, and compelling their respect. I ask you, therefore, Monsieur, and you, Madame, for an engagement of honor never to pick any of those roses. Your word will be sufficient for me'

"Seeing my wife moved, and that I was poorly disguising an anxious astonishment myself, he said: 'The property, as you are doubtless aware, belonged to Princess Tchersky.'

"He did not say anything more, either out of professional discretion or because he judged it unnecessary to tell us what everyone in Cannes knew about that subject, and limited himself to adding, by way of apology, while looking at the tips of his fingernails: 'The dead have strange caprices; as the living also have.'

"What could we do? My wife and I reflected until the following day; I interrogated various people, who responded evasively: 'Oh, yes, Princess Tchersky . . . Oh, yes, the roses . . .' Or, with a sort of regret: 'There's a beautiful view over the sea. It's said that the interior is very well fitted out; it's the princess's old furniture, nothing has been changed . . .' Or: 'Her daughter? We don't know. It's said that she lives in Vienna; she married the Duc d'Als, and never came back here . . .'

"The day after, we rented and entered into possession of the garden of roses. When I day *possession*, isn't that an irony, since it was under the prohibition to enjoy it other than by sight and smell? Personally, my God, it was indifferent to me whether or not I could pick the roses; I have always preferred living flowers on their stems; however, as every prohibition involves a humiliation and excites by reaction the temptation to break it, I felt—I don't know why—slightly vexed, discontented to have accepted such conditions. I dreaded above all that my wife might suffer from it more than me; that was, in fact, what happened.

"The next day we were walking in the bushiest part of the garden when, suddenly seized by one of those irresistible desires with which women are always pregnant, she extended her hand toward a beautiful rose.

"I said, mildly: 'Marthe!' She withdrew her hand meekly, but a minute later, I saw large tears in her eyes. She did not take long to pretext a migraine and to return to her apartment. At the point that her malady had reached, seeing her suffer was intolerable to me. I therefore headed for the back of the garden, where admirable crimson roses flourished, and, ashamed of breaking a word that I had given, but glad to give her pleasure, I cut twenty of those roses with a pen-knife, A shadow projected on the ground stopped behind me; the old gardener fixed reproachful eyes on me and murmured, with a sad and annoyed expression: 'That's forbidden.'

"I blushed like a child; I was in the wrong. I took a louis out of my fob pocket and tried to give it to the man, but he recoiled, shaking his head and repeated, almost angrily: 'That's forbidden.'

"Humiliated and irritated, I shrugged my shoulders and carried the flowers away. I avenged myself by thinking: *How ugly that old man is! What an unpleasant face! What harm am I doing? Anyway, it's too stupid!*

"'Here,' I said to my wife, depositing the roses in her lap. She didn't take them, or look at them, and the roses slid over her dress and fell on to the carpet. I picked them up and put them in a vase; but like Marthe, seeing them and respiring them didn't give me any pleasure; I experienced the petty sorrow that come from having acted badly, no matter how little harm one has done. I was therefore surprised when, three nights later, in admirable moonlight, my wife, who could not resign herself to going to bed even though the morning hour had already chimed, said to me seductively: 'It's so nice; shall we go for a walk in the garden? Well wrapped up, I promise you that I won't catch cold.'

"I opened the shutters of the glazed door to the veranda; the night was, indeed, warm, the sky swarming with tremulous stars; show gusts of air passed over the rose-bushes bathed in moonlight; their perfume was so strong and sweet that it drowned the heart in tenderness, desire and nameless, formless, colorless regrets, as poignant as a symphony heard with closed eyes. The roses, which we had not enjoyed, which had become foreign to us, which we almost disliked since the day of the bouquet, now attracted us, and we no longer felt the eye of the old gardener watching out for us. It seemed so different to us, without the illuminated sky, without the sun and without birds. It seemed, in the black peace of shadow and with the complicity of the moon, that the flower garden belonged to us, as to malefactors.

"I said to Marthe: 'Come!'

"What clarity there was, in the strange garden! One could see there as in broad daylight. Marthe, in her white dress, her pale face and her ash-blonde hair, seemed a being of light, a frail and supernatural phantom. Her lunar smile was, like that of children and invalids, as sad as it was charming, and it troubled my heart with obscure presentiments. Was she, in the environment of that night of flowers and stars, more conscious of the ephemerality of things and the brief existence that her illness was measuring? Or was it only the vague fears scattered in the darkness, the black forms of the unknown rooted in the thickets? Mystery enveloped us from all directions simultaneously; we both had a desire to turn back, but did not dare to; meanwhile, breaths of wind passed over our napes, and when the wind dropped, the leaves stirred singularly, without cause. A charm was floating.

"Marthe said to me: 'Smell, smell the roses!'

"What a subtle soul they exhaled, less strong than by day, in the sunlight, but more tender and more fluid, charged with unspeakable languor, a slight and penetrating fever—oh, penetrating all the way to the marrow! On the shadowed stems, outside the leaves that the moon tinted with vague sepia and fugitive verdigris, the white roses paled delightfully, along with the roses the color of a woman's flesh, the tea-roses, the straw-colored roses, while the red and garnet roses remained dark, like blood clots. But the bright roses, which one might have thought nude, surprised naked in their sleep, how vivid their suave gleams were, like delicate phosphorescences! We understood fully, Marthe and I, that we were walking in an enchanted garden!

"And, as if living and almost human voices were about to rise up by magic in the midst of the haunted pathways, as we approached the ponds and water features filled with aquatic plants at the rear, we heard a soft, sad song on two notes, one of them whistling and the other snoring: the melancholy song of toads. Clinging to my arm, with the invincible revulsion of women for crawling beasts, Marthe said: 'Let's go back, I'm afraid.'

"But then the enchantment that enveloped us took a new form. The shrill sound of a flute departed from who knows where, spacing out distant lulling modulations of a crude and bizarre caprice; around that invisible cadence, a great silence descended; the plaint of the toads had stopped, the rose garden seemed petrified; nothing could be heard any longer but the shrill crystalline notes of the instrument, falling like drops of water and beads of glass. Very close to us, a movement, and then another, and yet another agitated the leaves; a toad hopped out into the path, followed by a second. Was the charm of the flute attracting them? Now, formless, with low elastic leaps, an entire exodus of toads spread out into the damp moonlit pathway. I felt Marthe trembling in her every limb; fearfully, she breathed: 'Oh! Oh! Look!'

"The sound of the flute, which definitely seemed to be coming from behind the house, and which seemed to be causing the sad and rugged backs and the white goiters of the reptiles converge toward it, fell silent. Immediately, the exodus of the hopping population stopped. Flaccid bellies were inflated and, as if in response, the sad and grotesque love songs were croaked again. Then the flute resumed, but this time without interrupting them, and it was so unexpected, so magical and so moving, that crop of motionless roses, guarded by singing beasts, and the flute, that Marthe, seized by a sudden panic, fled toward the house, dragging me by the arm in a breathless and jerky run. But as we launched ourselves on to the perron, with the deliverance of people reaching port, my wife uttered a loud scream and recoiled. On the threshold of the glazed door, which I had left open, a toad was sitting gravely, gazing at us, barring our passage.

"With hasty strides, like a rescuer running in response to an appeal, crushing the gravel underfoot, we turned round, and saw the old gardener, the bizarre enchanter of the nocturnal garden, with a flute between his fingers, which he lifted like an orchestra conductor's baton over the toad. The beast then decided to go away; as if regretfully, it went down the steps

of the perron and we were able to return home, under
the grave gaze of the man, who waited for us to close
the door again. We had not exchanged a single word
with him, so much had those simple things—roses,
beasts and an old man playing the flute by night—elevated the sensation of mystery and the anguish of the
unknown.

"Marthe and I took a long time to go to sleep; our
insomnia remained agitated by occult, indiscernible
presences: the certainty that one has, in certain rooms,
of not being alone, without knowing whether it is the
life of things or an intrusion of spiritual beings that
makes those dubious effluvia and that sharp malaise
float around us. Suddenly, in the soft shadow and
the vague luminosity cast by a poorly-burning night-
light, I heard the click of teeth departing from the bed
backed up against the wall, near the door, on which
my wife was lying. 'Is that you, Marthe?' I exclaimed.

"She replied to me, in a halting and stammering
gasp: 'It's . . . it's me. I have . . . a fever'

"I was leaping out of bed when she cried: 'Stop!
Don't budge! Listen!'

"She had raised herself up on her elbow, and, shivering, her eyes blank: 'Stop breathing. Listen, listen . .
. that respiration! There's someone, someone under the
bed, someone in the room!'

"In fact, a slow and unusual, inexplicable sound, a
living breath, was rising and descending somewhere.
Who, then, could have slipped in through the door to
the perron, left open during our walk in the garden?
Already, with a lighted candle, my pocket revolver in

my hand, I was crouching before Marthe's bed. She repeated: 'Be careful. Oh! Oh!'

"But I saw nothing, nor anything under my bed, nor behind the sofa. The cupboards, devoid of depth, offered no refuge, but I opened them anyway; a screen in one corner might have hidden something; I unfolded its leaves abruptly, without result. And yet, the extraordinary respiration inflated jerkily, like that of a being who was hiding, and afraid. I started moving the armchairs. Suddenly, Marthe screamed, and a black form leapt on to the carpet: an enormous spotted toad that had been squatting behind a chair. I ran to the door in order to open it for the animal, but, frightened, it leapt toward my wife, who began uttering terrible cries, saying: 'Catch it! Catch it! Throw it outside!'

"That was easy to say, but my repulsion was no less than hers. I put my revolver—ridiculous, in the circumstances—on the mantelpiece and armed myself with a cane. The toad disappeared under an armchair; I chased it out; it bounded on to a chair; I herded it into a corner and, with a violent thrust of the stick released like a spring, I sent it as far as the threshold of the room; but instead of fleeing, it ran under Marthe's bed. She jumped down and ran to grab the bell-cord; she pulled it so forcefully that the cord broke and remained in her hand.

"The toad, hidden in a corner, refused obstinately to come out; lying flat, with the cane foraging under the bed, I tried in vain to find it and strike it; it played dead. The soft contact of its body descended to me from the tip of the cane in vibrations that made my hair bristle all the way to the fingernails. A rage gripped me; I pulled out the blade of the sword with which the stick was armed, and with all my strength I moved the bed aside in order to open up a passage. This time the toad moved; it hopped as far as the fireplace, burned itself there on the embers and leapt back on to the carpet. There was an idiotic and crazy pursuit until I succeeded in pinning it with the blade to the back of a low armchair. Its white abdomen deflated like a balloon; blood ran over the fabric; its paws parted frightfully, while its eyes appeared to spring forth from its head. The chambermaid, who came running, was just in time to catch Marthe in her arms; she was writhing in convulsions, and had to remain in bed for a fortnight, with fever and delirium."

De Vins fell silent for a moment, pensively, and then resumed:

"When my wife was able to get up she wanted to quit the villa at any price; to have changed rooms wasn't sufficient for her; like me, she saw the crucified toad again, with its stiff feet and its white belly spurting blood. It was, it appeared, according to the physician who was summoned during the night, a female, with an enormous belly. Doubtless it had been on the threshold of the perron with the male when our arrival, and that of the gardener, had made it flee. It had gone into the drawing room, and from there into our bedroom, the door of which, I remember, we had left open momentarily; for we were sleeping on the ground floor, the bedrooms above being too cold.

"So much for the material explanation. But the anguishing charm of that garden, the why of that troubling night, the stupefying fact that the beast had entered our home in order to scare us to death, and a thousand sensations that I cannot explain but which we experienced, which enveloped us by night with strangeness and malaise, dreams so mysterious, such a soft and enervating malaria, and by day with so many dead desires and illusory dreads, that luminous spleen the color of roses, and finally, the languorous nostalgia of dying—yes, everything that truly symbolized the haunted dwelling—shall I ever be able to explain that?

"It's true," he went on, "that when we had cancelled the lease, three weeks later, and had quit La Rosaire forever, people's tongues were loosened, and it was no longer hidden from us that Princess Tchersky had lived in that house insane for twenty years until her death, and that her son had blown his brains out. But what does that prove?"

And de Vins repeated slowly, in an unconvinced and hesitant manner: "What does that prove?"

TALES FOR A RAINY DAY

"A radiant sun bathed the gardens with gold, every leaf bearing a feather of light; the sky was nothing but a blue stream. The warmth was so intense that the turtle-doves were swooning on the rims of the marble basins. Princesse Epervière and Prince Grémit, swinging in the same silk hammock of rainbow-colored silk . . ."

Nothing is less true. It is raining abominably. It is three o'clock in the afternoon and it is necessary to light the lamp. If the shutters remain open it is because of a vain scruple, and in order not to lose the melancholy landscape that is blurred by a veil of water. The windows, vermiculated by raindrops, leave deformed foliages of transparency, undulating and parallel wakes of verdure. The wind is blowing and the branches are dripping tears. Two sounds alternate: the mousy squeaks of the trickling water and liquid fan-flicks of the wind. The fireplace is smoking.

"Princesse Epervière had the most beautiful hair in the world; Prince Grémit was the most handsome man in the kingdom. One could not see a better matched couple . . ."

A quill plied in the fingers is a strange thing, subjugating thought; it goes back and forth with a supple, magnetic fluidity. Only old quills are worth something. This one is new and devoid of finish. It squeaks imperceptibly on the paper. The noise is too faint for me to perceive it, but the cat has woken up; she is sitting up at the edge of the table, following with her eyes, whose pupils are thinned by the lamplight, the black furrow that the little pointed beak is tracing on the page.

Yes, Houppette—thus named because of your white robe, as soft and smooth as a swansdown powder-puff—that is the way it is. Listen carefully:

"Now, as the prince and the princesse were getting drowsy, enlaced with one another and mouth to mouth . . ."

Ah! That's what I feared, Houppette! Your grave green eyes, so mysteriously fixed on me, don't presage anything good. No, if you please! Come on, cat, I beg you! What diabolical sensuality do you find in parading yourself between my pen and my nose, offering me by turns, in accordance with the invariable custom of your peers, your pink muzzle and the star creased beneath your tucked-up tail. Why are you effacing the still-wet strokes of that phrase, and, as a sign of sovereign scorn, rubbing your backside over it, which retains a little ink?

"Get down, Houppette; this page is utterly spoiled!"

How it's raining! The muslin that covered the sky has become a sheet of gray canvas. The crepuscular daylight has the sadness of a winter dawn and kind of indecisive and suspect soul that leaves thought in suspense. One floats, as if exiled outside of things and outside of oneself. That doesn't resemble anything; it's stranger than dismal. The rain and the wind are fusing into a dull hum. Everything is gray. It's necessary, however, to write this tale. Let's try something else:

"Madame de Snobs turned on the hot water tap; from the silver swan's-beak the water gushed, splashing bubbles that evaporated the odorous surface of the water into vapor. The young woman felt warmed up, and splashed the warm wave over her throat and sides by moving her white hand back and forth. The silver swan had fallen silent, while she amused herself again, raising the milky sheet through which her body was opalized, with a rhythmic flux and reflux, merely by breathing forcefully; her delicate breasts emerged partly, and their pink nipples broke the surface."

Le's put some more wood on the fire. Let Madame de Snobs wallow in liquid warmth as much as she pleases! Let's extend our hands toward the dry, crackling flames and the rutilant velvet of the embers!

Sorry to disturb you, Houppette! How can you leave your muzzle in that furnace without the tip of your nose curling up like parchment? Oh, how that arched back pleases me! What a suggestion of a white dromedary in a sun-baked Sahara! Don't look at me like that, mewling, with plaintive eyes. Their green phosphorescence troubles me. Why do cats, without distinction of sex, have feminine gazes, and both dogs and bitches masculine gazes?

Meanwhile, the embers quiver with a furtive life; between the half-light that escapes and the semi-darkness the glides, they redden desirably with a vivid crimson that shifts, softening and sharpening; reflections dance and flee along their sparkling frame; one might think that blood were flowing and congealing from living ruby hearts or red suns. The lamp, in a dark corner of the room, casts its yellow fire. And the daylight tints the windows with a salty verdigris. The falling rain seems dirty. The earth is mud . . . everything is oozing like a wet sponge. "Rotten weather," as Ben Jonson said. Let's press on:

"Madame de Snobs was enjoying her idle wellbeing when she saw a shadow pass over the little window that overlooked the park, which stuck to the glass, ugly, flattened, wide-eyes, frightful and hairy; she perceived a human face that was contemplating her avidly, with the shining eyes and contracted and grimacing features of a faun. She stifled a cry of terror as she recognized Sambo, the huge orangutan, Monsieur Snobs' favorite, which he had brought back from his voyage to the heart of Africa: a terrible beast that was kept chained up, with an iron collar, since it had thrown itself upon a maidservant in order to violate her. Madame de Snobs stood up recklessly; at the same moment the glass shattered into splinters; the frame cracked, and the orangutan, passing through its head and its immeasurably long arm . . ."

Now there is a veil of ash and soot covering the world, for all the features of the landscape have disappeared, drowned and smothered by the dust, which is darkening by the minute. The lamp is burning more brightly, and the raindrops falling down the chimney are sizzling on the embers. Sad gleams are illuminating the windows of the neighboring houses—gleams that the wet glass magnifies into confused stars and troubled radiance, like a patch of ink on blotting-paper. Shutters are closing with soft grating sounds over the interior life of the people. A poor silhouette of a vagabond is going along the road, without even hurrying, heavy with the clinging rain and the sticky mud. A distress ring in the knell of the water and the soporific gasp of the wid. Dusk descends in a gradual thickening of the darkness, as if ink were being poured into the livid bath of the twilight.

It rains and rains!

This is not a time to tell stories but to listen to them. Magical print deploys its cabalistic characters better in such weather, in the lamplight. "My dear *Mille et une nuits!*" cried Alfred de Musset. It is pleasant to take refuge in dreams that cause life to be forgotten. And one would like to be a little child again in order for a grandmother, with her benevolent smile and her broken voice, which she punctuates with her short breath, to say to you:

"In those days, my dear boy, hens had teeth and guinea-pigs talked. This story happens in the land of fruit preserves. King Cédrat and Queen Amandedouce had no children, and they desired a little daughter passionately. The fay Carabosse, who was a wicked fay, had chilblains on her nose and calluses on her chin . . ."

Alas, the laurels are cut; there are no more grandmother's tales. The cat is ridding herself of fleas, ready for the feline sabbat. The lamp is burning in the dense night. The wood is sizzling.

"It's raining, shepherdess, it's raining!"[1]

---

1 "*Il pleut, il pleur, bergère*" [It's raining, shepherdess, it's raining], is a famous song from a comic opera, *Laure et Pétrarque* (1780), by Fabre d'Églantine; the reference in to Marie Antoinette, who, it is alleged, liked to dress up as a shepherdess in a private area of the gardens of Versailles, but the ideative link between the rain and the 1789 Revolution was only cemented with the aid of hindsight, when it was sung to celebrate the founding of the Garde Nationale. it was also alleged that Fabre d'Églantine hummed it when he was sent to the guillotine himself during the Terror in spite of having supported the Revolution. He had served as Georges Danton's secretary and had helped to name the months of the Revolutionary calendar. All that was doubtless in the back of the mind of the writer whose stream of consciousness is being explored.

THE BREATH

HENRY DE TRÈMES took the floor. With his back to the mantelpiece, he seemed very tall between two ardent bushes of candelabra. Nonchalantly, he respired a rose that Madame Any-Rolland had removed from her corsage in order to offer to him. They had just been talking about spiritism and had tried, without success, to make tables turn. An old lady, Comtesse de Mornelles, had told a rather troubling story of second sight. The bald Monsieur Rogat, full of self-importance, had affirmed that his wife, in the course of a nervous illness, had seen—distinctly seen, in the flash of a hallucination—their best friend, Monsieur de Bretache, who was dying at the same moment in Senegal. He had appeared to her in the middle of the drawing room, in a full dress uniform of an officer in the spahis. A credulous and polite silence had greeted that declaration; it made the pretty Madame Rogat blush and a few skeptics smile, who believed that they knew that Monsieur de Bretache had often entered her home in the flesh, for which reason there was no cause for astonishment if, regretting him so much, she had evoked him in his absence.

Henri de Trèmes spoke—and the moment was certainly appropriate for it, minds being turned toward mystery offering themselves to the acceptance of strange things: "For my part, I have always been refractory to the marvelous. Not that I'm simple-minded enough to think that our five limited and imperfect senses encompass the infinity that embraces us, but because, everything remaining surrounded by the unknown, our senses have habituated us to live in equilibrium with the material world and ambient spirituality, and any rupture of that equilibrium is thus dolorous. Either by virtue of habitude or decision, mostly by virtue of indifference, but also by virtue of fear of lifting the veil of mystery, we act, think and dream in the bosom of occult forces as if everything were explained and appears to us to be natural and normal.

"That is so true that we voluntarily expel painful thoughts from our route, like those of malady and death. We don't like to talk about them. If someone, in conversation, brings up those subjects, we quickly turn away and make appeal to more cheerful ideas. In the same way, we know very well that our crude senses only allow a feeble fraction of subterranean and invisible realities to reach us. We are not unaware that the prettiest little finger and the whitest woman's hand is, beneath its smooth and perfumed tissue, a frightful receptacle of voracious and monstrous lives; that the drop of the blood we suck so willingly if the thorn of a rose has caused it to spring forth, is a living liquid, a

Borgiaesque poison in which terrible animalcules hurl themselves upon one another. We know that, and yet we hasten to forget it, because such a discord between the real, such as it appears to us, and the real, such as science fashions it, is something painful, and an insupportable obsession.

"That is why, like many others, I avoid opportunities to break the precious equilibrium between our ordinary vision of things and the unusual aspect that the same things take on in the disquieting light of the marvelous. That advances nothing, teaches nothing, and only serves to make us more bitterly aware of the unfathomable darkness in which we move: bright and sunlit darkness, sometimes, like that in which a man can lose himself whose closed eyes see rosy fire, but darkness nevertheless.

"I don't deny anything, therefore. What do we know? Is not existence itself the most deceptive act. To think of nothing for a minute, to examine oneself, to see and hear oneself living, gives one vertigo. Only count to ten the palpitations of your being, trying to 'think of yourself,' fathoming the consciousness of your identity progressing toward death, and repeating to yourself: 'I'm alive, I'm me, I recognize myself: I'm alive, that's me, still me!' and an abominable anguish will circle your temples; you'll have a desire, in order to escape yourself, to scream; you'll sense yourself going mad.

"One lives without thinking about it. That's why we detest the boredom that forces us to graze upon our own substance, to chew the cud of our own emptiness. That's why certain splenetic contemplations are so terrible and why, having the horror of weaving for oneself, like a larva, a repugnant cocoon made of one's own soul, more than one person has killed himself in order to escape that torture.

"I don't, therefore, seek new sensations. Mine are sufficient for me. Rather, I fear the unknown. Are our poor nerves so resistant that they need further perturbation? Only once has a mysterious warning finger come to knock at my door. I did not summon the grave emotion that I felt and I did not try to retain it when its vibrations had dissolved in my being. I have not even sought to explain the event, in which one can see, as one chooses, a disquieting intrusion of spirit or a more-than-improbable coincidence.

"I was suffering then, in the sun of Cannes, from a long influenza, poorly treated, which had altered the functioning of my respiration and my heart. Nervous malaises, sudden oppressions and temporary congestions subsisted, although the cure was making considerable progress. It was just that the beautiful country in question—too beautiful, full of the effluvia of the sea and the hot sun, and also full of perfidious coolness after three o'clock— by virtue of its changing splendor, revived in me a state of feverish languor and nostalgia, prompt to tenderness and to the intimate sadness that radiant days engender.

"A letter had reached me during the day, informing me that a common friend of myself and the writer, a dear friend—you knew him Madame," de Trèmes put in, inclining toward Madame Any-Rolland—"a gallant man, an exquisite soul, Marc d'Aubanes, was dying in

Cairo, where, pretexting his health but in reality to flee an atrocious treason on the part of a woman, he had just been sent as a consul. There was no doubt for me that he was dying as much from the abandonment of that woman as from the malady of the heart by which he claimed to be afflicted. That news, which came after other letters less and less reassuring, distressed me more than it surprised me. I expected, alas, an imminent denouement. I anticipated that a telegram would inform me before long of the death of poor d'Aubanes.

"That day and the next went by without that cruel dispatch reaching me. Nothing signaled it except that I thought about my friend a great deal, remembering the pleasant hours of our affection, so many ideas exchanged and noble services rendered, a thousand petty events: a handful of ashes, still warm, that I raked with a profound melancholy. I went to bed mortally sad, and, I remember, the sight of a bouquet of violets in a glass of water on a table brought tears to my eyes.

"It was late when I went to sleep. My dreams were heavy and confused, oppressed by the menace of a vague peril, the apprehension of a nameless and formless misfortune. Suddenly, I awoke, or thought I awoke, with the clear sensation of a hand tugging the pillow under my head, with a slight shock, but without lifting it up. Shortly afterwards, although I can't measure the interval, another shock woke me entirely. The room was empty, and the night-light placed on the mantelpiece behind me projected the shadow of my head into the gap hung with white guipure curtains falling from the canopy of the bed.

"At first I remained under the influence of the strange seizure. The shock had been so precise that I retained a fearful stupor, my gaze searching every corner and covert of the room. No hand of flesh could have slid between the headboard of the bed and the wall. And yet, after that slight shock, an obscure fear gave me the sensation, the certainty, of the mystery that had entered the room. My ideas were galloping, prey to a panic flight. Then, suddenly, a singular serenity appeased the tumult of my heart, which had started to beat with great upheavals. I thought about d'Aubanes; I saw him dead and I said to myself: 'Is it him?'

"That was unreflective, unmotivated by anything, but the idea penetrated me to the utmost depths. I was no longer afraid; I was not even astonished; I communed with him in my heart and soul. Immediately, faint tremors, scarcely sensible gleams, were propagated over the walls and the furniture of the room. One might have thought that sparse, inconsistent whims of force were trying to live, to vanish in fluid waves. The entirely spontaneous idea occurred to me again that d'Aubanes, or the immaterial essence that had been liberated from his terrestrial body, had not been able to pull the pillow from beneath my head but had twice *alerted* me, at the base of the nape of my neck, like an electrified finger or the extremity of a conductive wire. As soon as the very gentle shocks shook my body, propagating in vibrations in my nerves and my bone-marrow, I had experienced the tremor that a weak electric discharge might communicate.

"The gleams still fluttering around the room were diminishing, however. Over time, the palpitating effluvia that were inundating my entire body were spaced out, fading away. Then a *breath* passed over my face and made the hairs stand on end: a cold breath, a breath that did not resemble any other, a breath of the beyond that congealed the blood in my veins with the frisson of death . . .

"The next day," de Trèmes said, after falling silent momentarily and passing his hand over his temples, with a gesture that was quite natural, but which seemed impressive, "a dispatch informed me that d'Aubanes had died during the night, and that he had pronounced my name in his death throes, and that of another friend, the painter Isidore T***.

"When I returned to Paris, that friend, while we were talking about d'Aubanes, let me tell him that adventure at length; then he seized me by the wrist and confessed that, almost at the same time, he had heard unusual creaks in the furniture. He had got up and had explored his apartment, thinking that thieves might be present. When he returned to his bedroom, a *breath* had blown out the lamp, which was still high and motionless, and that breath had also swept over his face and chilled his blood. At that moment, without any cause, without any preliminary association of ideas, he had thought of d'Aubanes and had said to himself that d'Aubanes, perhaps dead, was *alerting* him . . ."

THE THREE PHANTOMS

His body free in loose garments, Pierre, lying on the divan, is following the blue meanders of idle cigarette smoke, Between the pale green blinds of study, decorated with green and white English fabrics and water colors, a little fresh air enters, with the noise of the avenue, the clip-clop of hooves and the rumble of wheels. A delicate odor of vervain is evaporating. Pierre's eighteen years are dreaming about amour.

That magical word wakes infinite prolongations in his soul: the marvelous unknown real has neither a commencement nor an end. And Pierre sighs after the enchanted land. A desire, sometimes languid and sometimes keen—a vast desire, quivering like a polar wind, which carries the odor of forests, rivers, seas and mountains—assails and stirs him. Amour! A profound, unfathomable word, terrible and yet so sweet! Floating forms, essences of women, fluid gazes, smiles that retain a little of the sky, gestures that have a soul, and the impalpable flower of the ideal flesh of the visage, the hands, the nape of the neck, the shoulders, nacreous seed, naked fruit!

Amour! Hope, anguish, doubt, dolor, intoxication, agonizing jealousy, mortal treason, bitter and delectable remorse; one would like to live ten lives; one would like to die; one devours space, one suppresses time; one is a beast or a god; all saps and all forces flow within you, and for an instant, one believes oneself to be immortal.

Pierre dreams and summons amour—which he does not know—with all his being. How will it come to him? A timid girl whose eyes open like two somber little pansies? A plump courtesan with transparent veils and painted eyelashes and cheeks? A perverse and ingenuous woman of the world, symbol of elegance and luxury? A gypsy with coppery cheeks and cold hands that burn? A pauperess of the highway? A sweet blonde bourgeoise of a little town in Germany, all beer and milky coffee?

And Pierre suspends his desire over the women he knows: those who have looked at him, smiling; those who have drawn away without seeing him; those who pass by in carriages like queens; those who prowl the streets, shamefully; those who toil every day in humble tasks; young women who give the impression of mocking him; mature ladies, still beautiful who show an interest in him.

None of them personify, for him, Amour in its entirety.

Then he evokes phantoms, more real than reality, more alive than life. those who are not born of the flesh but of the soul of a man, those into whom a spiritual creation has breathed the fire follet that animates them. the heroines, the divine lovers! They are innumerable. There is not one of whom he has not dreamed, with a troubled heart, in the tenderness of long evenings, to whom he has not appealed in the insomnia of his solitary bed, whom he has not seen vanish in the morning sunlight. The nymph Eucharis, the crescent Diana, Venus in her chariot drawn by doves, you, suave La Vallière, you, Faust's Marguerite; and, holding one another by the hand, the three dolorous Graces, daughters of the three great novelists of the century—Balzac, Stendhal and Flaubert—emerge fully alive, entirely ardent, from the three crucibles of human thought, *Le Lys dans la vallée*, *Le Rouge et le noir* and *L'Éducation sentimentale*: Henriette de Mortsauf, Madame de Renai and Madame Arnoux.

Pierre feels his eyes moistening and his heart in tumult. Dear phantoms, exquisite phantoms, whom he has only clasped in an imaginary embrace, only possessed in an intoxication of the soul! How he loves them, with a fervor sometimes humble and sometimes imperious, but always passionate to the point of fainting! They are propitious to him, and also benevolent. They hear the stifled cry that he murmurs toward them; they have understood the irresistible impulse that lifts him toward their murderous mouths and their plaintive eyes—so pure, all three, Madame de Mortsauf and Madame Arnoux, the inviolate, and Madame de Renai, perhaps even greater than them because she has give herself and has wept blood.

By an insensible transformation, the protean soul of youth, the supple and volatile imagination that condenses in a thousand diverse forms, Pierre loves, at this moment, Madame de Mortsauf. Timid, adolescent, taking refuge in a corner, he sees her in the tumult of the fête, sit down next to him. A perfume intoxicates him. His eyes are suddenly struck by the plump white shoulders on which he would have liked to fall, the slightly pink shoulders that seem to be blushing, as if they were finding themselves naked for the first time: "modest shoulders that had a soul, whose satin skin shone with light like silken cloth." He raises himself up, palpitating, in order to see the bodice, and remains fascinated by a "cleavage chastely covered by gauze, but of which the blue-tinted globes of a perfect roundness were softly couched in floods of lace." And now the beautiful book deploys its pages, showing him at every moment, in a nimbus of memory, a glory of adoration, Madame de Mortsauf, with her undulating voice of a golden timbre, the voice that "understood the meaning of words and drew you into a superhuman world," with her fine ash-blonde hair, her rounded forehead, as prominent as that of La Gioconda, her green-tinted eyes speckled with brown dots, her ever-pale eyes whose sudden light, in joy or in pain, "seemed to catch fire at the wellsprings of life and ought to dry them up." Soul of renunciation, smile of silence sand solitude, the beautiful lily of the valley flowers, withers and dies. And Pierre has her last gaze, her last smile.

Another phantom glides into the room, light and furtive. Fully adorned with her provincial grace, it is that Madame de Renai, who seemed "a woman of thirty, but still quite pretty," so proud and so naïve, so delicate and so pious, whose education "was made by dolor," and who loves with so much sincerity, so much ardor, so much remorse; who pales and blushes while, so pretty in her light new summer dress, dressed in everyday stockings and little shoes from Paris, she attaches her eyes anxiously to the *enfant terrible* who is Julien Sorel. How charming she is in the transports, so sincere, of her amour, and in the despair, so sincere, of her sin! With what burning sensibility she believes herself to be redeemably damned, and seeks to hide the sight of Hell while heaping Julien with the most ardent caresses! Pierre sees, in its length and breadth, the cruel and sweet book, substitutes himself for the egotistical, willful and passionate hero. With what anguish, with what a heart in suspense, he sets the ladder against Madame de Renai's window, raps on the pane, perceives, like a white shadow, "a shadow that seemed to be advancing, with an extreme slowness, a cheek that was applied to the window." Afterwards, however, he no longer has the courage to follow Julien as far as his vengeance and his attempted murder; he wants to forget, to remain in the divine night of reproaches, tears, despair and kisses. And the light white phantom escapes and vanishes.

The third adorable woman appears, the placid and noble bourgeoise with her discreet and penetrating charm, nearer to us, more lifelike and less ideal, but who is irresistibly seductive: the Madame Arnoux to whom Frédéric will make, later—too late—as one spreads incense at the foot of an urn of ashes, the unforgettable declaration: "Your person, your slightest movements, seem to me to have an extraordinary importance in the world. My heart, like dust, rises up behind our footsteps, You have the effect on me of moonlight on a summer night, when all is perfume and soft shadows. Whiteness, space, and the delights of the flesh and the soul are contained for me in your name, which I repeat, savoring a kiss on my lips!" Tender, serious and so good, Pierre cannot think of her without being softened by a sweetness; he sees her, for the first time, on the deck of the boat, with Frédéric's eyes, and she is like an apparition in her large straw hat, the pink ribbons of which flutter in the wind behind her. Her black hair tuning around the tips of her large eyebrows, descends very low and seems to be pressing the oval of her face amorously. Her straight nose, her chin, and her entire person, are outlined against the backcloth of the blue atmosphere. What a melancholy tenderness it is that, throughout a book, throughout a life, will unite Pierre—no, Frédéric—and Madame Arnoux, but it is Frédéric, not Pierre, who understands her and loves her in "that August of women when the force of the heat is mingled with the experience of life and, at the end of its expansion, the complete being overflows with riches in the harmony of its beauty." And she too draws away, dissolves into the sadness of the dusk. And Pierre is alone; he thinks about the vanished women.

Poor Madame Arnoux, poor Madame de Renai, poor Madame de Mortsauf, eternally sacrificed to the mediocrity of marriage, to down-to-earth existence, profound hearts in which amour has opened like a beautiful fruit and closed again without having ripened! Pierre thinks about the three phantoms, who are not only ideal, imaginary and delectable mistresses; no, those three women are more and better, the inspiration of his solitude and the noble advisors of his thought. They teach him, by their renunciation, and by their grandeur, to flee vulgarity, baseness and mediocre pleasure. They turn away from hard, dry or simply and grossly egotistical faces, husbands who love them poorly and cannot comprehend them, lovers who are truly inferior to them; they surround Pierre with their floating and invisible scarves, drawing him toward a world of superior aspiration where, thanks to them, in memory of and out of respect for them, he will want more and will rise higher. For they are the Three Graces of dolor, the Three grave and tender Muses, the advisors and initiators of pure amour.

LEGENDS

THE STONE OF THE DWARFS

OBSCURE life of the depths of the soul! Mysterious memory! In the busy hours of a day spent searching, in the Algiers to which I have returned, for an apartment in which to work tranquilly, with windows overlooking the hillside and the bay, why have I started thinking melancholically of other countries, of places that I do not know, of distant lands of mist?

Far from here, far from this city, always dear to me, with its white houses and the blue sea, I have been dreaming since this morning of childish stories, of evenings of wind and rain in Cornouailles, on the heath amid the gorse. And since night is falling, since the blazing fire and the lighted lamp make the room less hostile—the hotel room with walls seemingly impregnated with foreign existences, the sad room in which others have lived, slept and loved—the hour that is chiming seems to me to be the signal for departure. Let's go. if you wish, toward the desert plain and the mountains of Arrée. Here is the old legend as it was related to me on one of those late evenings before Breton fireplaces where woman still tell the old tales.

*

In those days, near the confluence of the Elez and the Aune, on one of the foothills of the Black Mountain, the Château de Timeur raised its nine towers against the open sky. Above them, at the level of the keep, a golden banner fluttered in the wind. It was there that the very noble and powerful knight Guillaume de Rosmandec lived, with his daughter Alice.

Alice had grown up, motherless—for Madame de Timeur had died giving birth to her—the unique thought of the aged seigneur. She was dearer to him than the manor of his ancestors and the gold heaped up in his coffers. And, thinking that the moment would soon come of her betrothal and departure, he lamented in his heart; he could have wished that, by means of a magical sleep, the present hour might be eternalized for him.

The glory of Kadoc, the son of the Seigneur de Prat-Thule, in the parish of Cléden-Poher, was well known. He was one of those knights whom beauties did not disdain. Alice was not unaware that, among all those who broke lances in the tourneys then held by Charles de Blois of the duchy of Bretagne,[1] Kadoc had won great renown, and when they saw one another, the virgin's breasts palpitated within her tight bodice. But did the young chatelaine know what it cost to be the lady of Timeur? Did she imagine that the heritage

---

1 Charles de Blois-Châtillon, Duc de Bretagne (1319-1364).

of her domain, the long mantle of blazoned ermine, would weigh so heavily on her frail shoulders?

"My daughter will only marry a very rich lord, and I believe that fortune has smiled upon you less thus far than glory, Messire Kadoc." And as the adolescent knight lamented, attesting imminent days, Guillaume escorted him back to the portcullis, pointing with his finger at the black line of woods that closed the horizon. "Unless the forest of Kerun yields its treasures to you, and its jealous guardians the korrigans, who dance around their sacred stone in the evening, welcome you into their rounds."

Time has passed. A fine rain is striping the sky interminably and great clouds run over the heath, where the wind whistles through the granite rocks and the prickly gorse. Today, through the open door of a low chapel, a deacon has blessed the growling departure of dogs on leashed and impatient horses. Now, the hunt is galloping through the woods of Kerun. Stags, wolves and wild boar scatter. Dusk has fallen while the horn was still sounding, and in the ruddy light and smoke of torches the hunters are galloping through the terrible forest. Then all clamors die away.

The Chevalier de Rosmadec is lying in a clearing. He has lost touch with the hunt; he is asleep, leaning against a standing stone. The great confused trees are entwining their motionless masses. An enormous moon has risen; it is bleeding into the opaque fog.

Wake up, handsome knight. Around the sacred stone a multitude of little creatures is whirling, with enormous ugly heads, bearded and grimacing.

Guillaume de Rosmadec is on his feet. He is holding his spear in one hand, and draws his sword with the other. He tries to break the magic circle. The spear shatters and the sword breaks. The round is still turning. Then a dwarf smaller than all the others emerges in front of the knight and says to him, with the voice of a cricket, smiling in a diabolical fashion:

"Chevalier de Rosmadec, you have slept in the shadow of our stone and you have tried to attack us. You know, however, what danger there is merely in passing through this clearing, where our treasures are buried. Others have been drawn into our eternal dance for less. Depart, you are free; only you will bring us, in a year's time, the first woman who pours you a drink. Adieu; fear the vengeance of the dwarfs."

And as Guillaume opened his mouth, everything disappeared. There was no longer anything in the clearing but the mysterious stone extending its shadow over the grass, the bloody disk of the moon and the motionless mass of great confused trees. Then Guillaume went home, at a slow pace.

In the Chevalier de Rosmadec's bedroom the lamp has gone out. Alice is sitting by the bed. She is gazing, without seeing them, at the long tapestries in which characters from fable seem possessed of a strange life, illuminated momentarily by dancing gleams.

Feverish words in an agitated sleep: "A drink! A drink!"

And when Guillaume wakes up, he perceives with terror the empty cup in Alice's hand.

It is necessary to live with the terrible thought. Time does not pause in its slow march, and the sand always flows inexorably through the hour-glass. Spring passes, summer expires and winter returns. Then Guillaume sets forth on the pilgrimage of Saint Herbot.

The bells sound gaily in the campanile. White blouses and blue britches, in honor of the Pardon, fill the little church whose walls are covert with the tails of oxen and cows. But while the crowd presses around the statue of the saint, imploring the multiplication of bulls, the chevalier descends into a nearby grotto. Since time immemorial a solitary old man has lived there; he is a kind of sorcerer whose age and origin are unknown. Clad in an animal-skin cloak, he lives motionlessly in the middle of a magic circle that he had traced with his hazel-wood wand.

For a long time they remained together, but when Guillaume de Rosmadec emerged a mad joy shone in his eyes; he was laughing at the dwarfs. He was clutching a marvelous talisman to his chest.

Noël! Noël! The bells are ringing in the darkness, announcing the birth of the savior of the world. Snow is falling, the north wind whistling through the black branches. Who is running like that in the desolate heath? Snow is falling; only the howling of wolves rises up in the silence. Who is running like that through the standing stones toward the woods of Kerun? Is it some pious peasant hurrying to worship the infant Lord on Christmas Eve? Snow is falling, the forest is lamenting in the whistling wind. It is a white form; a fire follet is guiding it across the hardened snow, through the falling snow that is accumulating in the brushwood. Who would recognize the beautiful Alice de Rosmadec? Her unbound hair is floating in the wind. Her white dress has been lacerated by the thorn-bushes; her blue and golden shoes are torn by stones. Where is she running like that? The illuminated towers of Carhaix and Plouguer are extinct on the horizon. An owl emits its ululation; death-candles are lit behind the forest of Helgoat; the sound of the nocturnal laundresses is audible on the river.

She is going to join Kadoc; the korrigans have taken him away. In vain she has put the talisman given to her by her father around her neck, on the string from which the magic nut is suspended. Here is the clearing, and the peulven on which Kadoc is leaning. The infernal round is circling him.

"Enter into the dance, my beautiful bride," says the dwarf with the voice of a cricket. "The treasures are yours, you are going to be happy in our empire; Kadoc is our friend.

And while the white swan throws its lugubrious cry through the fog, Alice enters into the round. But the string breaks, the nut falls, and Alice and Kadoc disappear into the gulf that opens, amid the marvelous gold and the enchanted gems.

Then the furious gallop of a horse resounds. Around the sacred stone the korrigans are still dancing.

"Chevalier de Rosmadec," says the smallest of the dwarfs, "you have kept your promise; your daughter is ours."

And abruptly the stone falls, crushing the chevalier; a squall of snow passes, and only a few fire follets are still circling in the clearing, while the bells ring out over the plain to salute the birth of the divine child.

THE SENSUAL LOVERS

THE amour that burned Perlides and Nymphale no ice could extinguish; to satisfy their hunger and their thirst they needed no meat or drink; their illness was a torturing and exquisite wellbeing for which the physicians could find no remedy.

After the day when their mouths had mingled for the first time, to the song of the nightingale, while the petals of almond-trees snowed upon them, intoxicated by the kiss that their souls aspired, in which their flesh dissolved, they only lived in order to renew their ecstasy. The intrigues of the court and the inimity of their parents traversed their amour in vain; nothing prevented them from joining their lips again and fainting in one another's arms, until it was necessary to resolve to unite them by marriage.

From then acute desire that rendered them pale and ringed their beautiful eyes gave way to a sacred delight. They walked like gods; their smiles were not of this world. Whoever discovered, in the depths of the royal park, the white tunic of Perlides, distinguished almost immediately the soft floating cloud of Nymphale's robe. They were scarcely more separate than two turtle-doves flying in a pair, touching bills under a tree and going to sleep with the head of the female under the wing of the male.

One might have believed that possession would sate their souls, but there was nothing of the sort. The more they loved one another, the more they experienced the joy of the embrace, penetrating them and impregnating them with sensuality. Sometimes they remained shut in their room all day with the curtains closed, prolonging the flame of oil lamps. Sometimes, having retreated to a corner of the park so solitary that the hinds did not flee at their approach, they celebrated the mysteries of triumphant amour, bathing in streams of fresh water, enlaced in roses, or hidden in the cool shade of grottoes.

Contemplating one another was a source of infinite delight for them. Perlides held Nymphale seated on his knees; she tipped her head back under the ardor with which he darted his tongue over her teeth, and she swooned with a sigh while he squeezed her fingers. Then he rendered homage to the swollen rosebuds of her breasts; he called them by dear names, and like a child rocked by a nurse he savored their fresh and rosy aroma, the slightly bitter perfume of almond. Then he prostrated himself before her beauty, circling her waist with his arms.

She lifted him up and threw herself against him. She caressed the down of his cheeks and the roundness of the muscles of his arms. A force bound them together and bent them; they panted and sighed, laughed and wept, carried away by a crazy torrent; their pleasures resembled a wrestling match, or a grim pugilism; they rolled on the moss narrowly conjoined, their limbs entangled; and there was a relaxation in which all their happiness still palpitated, a delightful agony that did not want to die, faint smiles succeeded by silences so full that the soul overflowed with it like an over-full cup.

So strong was their need to augment the infinity of their intoxication that they would have liked to associate nature entire with it; when they reposed under the fraternal gaze of flowers in a soft enlacement they wanted to expand in the mildness of milk; they were almost astonished not to turn green and cover themselves with leaves in the ardent jet of the sap that flowed within them. It seemed to them that the majesty of the night, the magnificence of the stars, the glory of sunlit days and the crimson of the dawn became part of them and prolonged their being in all directions, into space.

There was, for them, no sensuality comparable to that procured for them by a bath of fresh water. A little of their consciousness scattered in the thousand fleeting ripples; their flesh flowed in the liquid reflection of shadows; lightened of human weight, they floated side by side, mingled with the fluid element, subtilized and almost liquefied. They were the singing stream; and embracing with soft arms, escaping in languid flights, they savored an ineffable sensation, vanishment into the great All, a death that was the supreme life.

But they appreciated no less the sensuality the refined sensualities of swimming baths and steam baths, the mollifying effect of warm water, the diffusion of sweat, the abrupt retreat all the way to the roots of the fibers of a body doused with seething icy water, in which their flesh, emerging from soft and caressant massages, retained an elastic delicacy, a new and infantile purity. Ingenious in discovering and varying anything that could stimulate their tenderness, they knew the sweetness of bathing in milk, and the intoxication of bathing in acrid and fuming wine.

They bathed in roses. Shredded into supple and odorous masses, they collapsed beneath them, in a crush of perfume and honey; there were pink baths smoother than silk, baths of a rich dark velvet, baths the color of sulfur and baths the color of flesh. And they also bathed in vertiginous carnations and in modest violets.

They bathed in oil of nard, wrestling thereafter in the fashion of slippery eels; they bathed in saffron, which made amber statues of both of them, and in crimson, which stained them with blood. They bathed in the white down of swans, which, sticking to their skin, mutated them into great bizarre birds, as if they had been born in unknown isles.

One day, playfully, in the manner of strolling players, they bathed in flour, rubbing their faces with it and laughing as they gazed at one another.

And they bathed in the straw of barns, the hay of ricks, the oats of horse-troughs. They bathed in gold coins that encrusted their limbs with effigies and figures. They emerged from water to bathe in fine sand, buried as far as the neck, savoring in advance, immobilized, the repose of believing themselves interred together.

It was thus that they married, not only one another, but all living and inanimate things, bathing in autumn in fallen yellow leaves that rustled and creaked, bathing in winter in the furs of dead beasts, the warmth of which smelled wild, and even bathing—O delirium!—in virgin snow that the ardor of their tenderness caused to melt around the form of their bodies.

Nymphale died.

She died with a smile, suddenly, without a cause, as they were listening to meadow-frogs sing by night. She was lying against a birch tree, her hand in Perlides'. She did not slide to the ground; her hand merely shuddered. She was still smiling, exactly similar to the minute before.

Except that she was dead.

Perlides built a great pyre with his own hands, deposited the body of his beloved upon it, set fire to the scented cedar wood and lay face down on Nymphale's body. in order that the last bath in which their love would unite them with the rest of the world, and dissolve them into things, would be both a bath of flames and a fulgurant symbol of their inseparable, unique and prodigious happiness.

Thus Perlides and Nympale, the sensual lovers, loved one another and were united for the last time.

A powerful wind, which seemed to be bemoaning their fate, sprang up when the fire was consumed, and dispersed their ashes in the sky and over the earth.

THE RED MOUNTAIN

THE RED MOUNTAIN! As the diligence, jolting over the absence of the road that once led to Biskra, set us down at the foot of a hill, we looked around. The immense ravined plain extended as far as the eye could see; to the right, the somber curtain of the oasis ringed the mountains of El-Kantara, and the gorges resembled a hole hacked out by gigantic blows of an ax. The Zibans drew their fleeting blue lines in the distance, and alone to our left the harsh ridges of the Red Mountain loomed up against the unalterable azure of the sky; it was as if the steep walls and sheer slopes were tinted crimson by ancient bloodshed.

"A strange place!" I said to Ben Salem, my traveling companion.

He nodded his head and, like all Arabs, full of superstition for things past, he told me the old legend perpetuated there, to the monotonous rhythm of guttural songs.

One day, long ago, Salah, a rich man and a son of glory, stepped on to that mountain, and resolved to plant his tents there. Spring was nascent, a thousand aromatic plants were exhaling a strong odor, and in the distant esparto-grass, already green, gazelles were leaping joyfully.

The next day, life went on. The flocks descended to the plain, and from his tent, Salah contemplated the innumerable livestock in the distance. Tribal chiefs passed by, their hands on their hearts, praising God; and Salah responded with a few wise words. Laughter rises from neighboring tents. That laughter was his life, his youth and his joy. Salah was the master of the hour, the son of Allah; and Kradidja was Salah's daughter.

Their days flowed by under the sun like a fortunate river. In the morning, the agha departed. Under the whitening sky that was about to be invaded by the dawn, the hunt galloped for a long time.

In the meantime, Kradidja directed the work of her women. They rolled the couscous into granules on large hurdles, and threw a ball to one another from the two corners of the frame on which wool was being woven.

Kradidja went out too. Camels knelt down before her, and she climbed on to the back of a white *mehari*. The deformed beasts swung their heads, causing a kind of palanquin to pitch, and white plumes floated above the *basseur* draped with dark cloth, from which a long amulet hung down all the way to the ground.

In front marched a young man of tall stature named Bou-Asfer; his duty was to watch over the women and to accompany them; he was Salah's favorite servant.

Having arrived at the tent, the camels knelt down. Kradidja stood up, very slim. The slave extended his hands, and as she leapt to the ground their trembling fingers touched.

✻

Toward the end of autumn, the agha, worried by his daughter's lassitude and her plaintive expression, searched suspiciously for the cause of that strange behavior.

Meanwhile, time marched on, and every minute, which augmented the agha's suspicion, fortified the obscure amour of the young people. Like a vivacious tree, it had driven its roots throughout their young hearts.

That evening, Kradidja and Bou-Asfer were chatting together on the part of the mountain where the descent is sheer. The moonlight tinted the plan blue in the distance; palm trees were outlined in black, and no wind was blowing through their motionless palms.

Sitting on an uprooted tree trunk, they were talking about the cruel life that had caused them to be born so far apart from one another. Their hands were joined, and on the bosom of the slave Kradidja was gazing at him, her soul entirely in her eyes.

Abruptly, however, her eyes widened, fixed with terror. Salah surged forth. With a single thrust, he drove a long dagger between Bou-Asfer's shoulders, crying frantically: "Die, dog! Dog of a slave!"

And, dragging the cadaver to the rim of the ravine, he cut its throat. When his daughter appeared, he swung the severed head in the air and threw it far away.

✳

After that, Salah received messengers from Taieb-ben-el-Hadj, who offered a very rich dowry in exchange for Kradidja. Salah, hateful against his daughter and desirous of getting rid of her, consented to the marriage. Tiaeb immediately sent weapons, Asian silks and horses harnessed with gold.

Kradidja was unaware of all that. Wrapped up in herself, she was living with her memory. Her life went by on a narrow mat; she curled up there, next to a tripod covered with embers, at which she stared incessantly.

One morning in spring, Taieb-ben-el-Hadj appeared. Flute-players and musicians striking long drums preceded him. Large banners of blue and yellow silk unfurled joyously. He was mounted on a white horse with wide palpitating nostrils, which he caused to prance on the spot. Servants surrounded him. He dismounted, kissed Salah on the shoulder, and they headed for the prepared tent.

They gathered around an immense tray, and twenty dishes filed past: lamb with eggs; filleted and mashed pâtés, meat with quinces and couscous. Then a slave brought an entire roasted sheep in his extended arms.

The instrumentalists played a lively tune, and fireworks burst forth. A fantasia commenced. The banner-carriers saluted at the gallop, sweeping the ground with floating silks. Intoxicated by the howls and the odor of gunpowder, the riders continued frenetic maneuvers to the sound of the drums and flutes.

But piercing cries rang out, and a woman came running, with distressed servants. Kradidja had just hurtled herself into the abyss where Bou-Asfer's head had tumbled from rock to rock.

When Salah and Taieb came running, haggardly, they contemplated a long trail of crimson blood, and, at the bottom of the ravine, a whiter form stained with red.

In the midst of the distressed silence of the men and the lamentations of the women, Taieb understood. He was not consoled for having been duped; filled with anger, he reproached Salah for his baseness in a low voice. And, black with rage, he cried to the agha, who had followed him:

"You shall not sleep in the cemetery of your fathers, turned toward Mecca and the rising sun!"

That same evening, with his horsemen and all the sound men of his tribes, he returned. Before Salah had time to put himself on the defensive, Taieb was in his doars. The livestock was taken, the women and children bound with cords. And as Salah fought valiantly at the head of all those that he could assemble, a bloody fever took possession of everyone. The rifles were abandoned; there was a long melee, an unspeakable hand-to-hand battle. It was then that Salah perished, obscurely, with all his race.

Taieb's horse, and those of his relatives, marched over a road of cadavers. The tents and the gardens were burned; everything that had the name of human was massacred; and blood flowed in abundance from the heights of the mountain, streaming in little cascades; when the sun set, the sheer walls and the rocks of the ravine were crimson.

The next day, Taieb departed again with his tribes, leaving to wild beasts the care of making everything that had lived there disappear. Soon, only a few blanched bones signaled that adventure, until, returned to its original sterility, the mountain outlined its harsh crests, bloody henceforth, against the azure as before.

"Your legend, Ben-Salem," I said, after a silence, "proves once again the wisdom of songs. One must not contradict amour."

He replied: "What God has resolved to accomplish, is always accomplished. Allah be praised!"

THE GUARDIAN OF BAD DREAMS

For Stéphane Mallarmé

THE KING OF THE LAKES was prey to nightmares; that was an evil spell cast on him by the Nixies when he caught one of them in the deployment of a spavin with crimson mesh weighed with silver quoits. The captive nixy struggled like a fish, her eyes already vitreous, and her woman's face and body of green scales resolved into the soft gelatin of a medusa. She melted in his hands and spread out in the grass, so rapidly diminished that she could not be seized, and flowed away in a ray of sunlight.

Since then, black or bloody nightmares assailed the king who violated the treaty; and he feared sleep as much as death. He stayed awake long after nightfall and only went to sleep to the sound of crystal flutes; brass horns woke him up at dawn. He no longer ate fish, nor hare, nor pâtés; those dishes made his soul too heavy; he no longer drank flame-colored wines, the intoxication of which was bitter and troubled. He even renounced brown narcotics, which plunged him into a bottomless Lethe, for his tomorrows took the place of nights, and it was then awake, with his eyes wide open, that the worst dreams haunted him, to such an extent that he lived them, by necessity, mouth agape, like a man afflicted by stupor; a cold sweat, similar to tears, ran down his cheeks.

The king, who no longer went to bed without the light of several candelabra, in a room fanned by clusters of ostrich plumes, on a bed as fresh and soft as fruit pulp, took it into his head to be woken up by a very old woman, so old that she had not slept for ten years, and who scared children with her hollow and vigilant eyes, in which a perpetual insomnia burned. He appointed her the guardian of his dreams.

Leaning over his face, she was to look out for somber reflections therein, the anguish that palpitates behind the eyelids, the unuttered screams that freeze upon the lips, signs more fleeting but no less revealing than sighs, moans and inconsequential speech. In doubt, for all the more reason, if she suspected his slumber, she was to extract him from it by placing her hand on his arm. And if she perceived that he was having lascivious dreams, she was to wake him up very rapidly, for such phantasms are followed by regrets.

She installed herself on a low seat beside the bed, and the king, after having turned from one side to the other for a long time, went to sleep.

He then descended into a well of shadow, and his entire body seemed to fall gently into a void. Floating, disparate images fulgurated before his eyes, and he found himself on a heath at twilight; the sun, low on the horizon, sent forth a pale light. He walked, and his shadow stretched out immeasurably, raised on stilts.

While walking he turned his head anxiously. A causeless anguish invaded him. He tried to explain it. Doubtless he had reached the limits of his kingdom, unknown lands where silver fountains sprang forth and crystallizing liquids solidified into stalactites of all colors. The nixies did not live there, but redoubtable spirits that growled under the earth spat out jets of vapor and hot mud. The king was still walking and hot lava burned the soles of his feet. He would have liked to pick a flower or to see an eagle fly, but it was a dead land. An infinite lassitude oppressed him, and the consciousness of mystery and fear penetrated him.

A large pond in the form of a seashell stopped him, from which hardened liquid had overflowed in pink and green drool. The bottom of the pond could not be seen, and the emerald liquid that filled it seemed to be boiling, for it was agitated by a continuous frisson. The king had stopped, and from foot to head his shadow was projected into the water, a brightly colored shadow that simulated life convincingly. He gazed at it, motionless, and it seemed to him that when the water froze in winter his own reflection would be frozen in it, soon thickened, dense and compact, petrified as a statue. By moving, he would doubtless have broken the charm and deformed the rigid resemblance, but it was impossible for him to stir his little finger; and from one second to the next, his double, the king of crystal, congealed into stone, while around him the water remained fluid and retained its soft tremor. His terror increased. He divined—yes, he knew, clearly—that the maleficent spirits of the ground were on the lookout for him. Where to flee? Would the image not attest that he had passed that way? He wanted to destroy it, to strike it with his foot, but he felt that foot, seized by the water-fay, stiffening fearfully, like sap rising in the pores of a tree; the liquid stone reached his leg, his thought and his entire body. He was going . . .

The old woman shook him. The king's wrath was great, because she was so late pulling him out of that Gehenna. But she swore a great oath that he had never had such an even respiration and a visage as calm, so that she had only woken him regretfully, and rather with excessive zeal.

After which, having proffered terrible threats, he went back to sleep.

Now he was walking in a strange garden, where nothing flourished but eyes. Enormous white bulbs stuck out everywhere on long and frail peduncles, and in the midst of those bulbs, which resembled tulips that must have flowered in the ground, with their onions in the air, an immense flower-bed radiated in all directions, formed of circles of green, blue, brown, yellow and violet irises striped with gold and jasper, with black pupils in the middle. And all those living eyes, in which one discerned male and female gazes, the gazes of ancestors and the gazes of newborns, those of cruel cats, affectionate dogs, piercing lynxes, yellow owls and dull fishes, all those eyes, in the envelope of the sclerotic, gave the impression of sick children swaddled in white.

The king engaged in sandy pathways, and under his footfalls the eyes blossomed; some leaned over on their stems as his cloak brushed them. Many greeted him with a reproach, a smile or a malediction. There were chaste ones and provocative ones, churlish ones and demented ones, and those of beasts contained an intense mute dream. A tenacious haunting! The king would have liked no longer to be harassed by those thousands of pupils; he fled, but the maze of eyes opened before him, innumerable and renascent. By mistake, he crushed one of the bulbs and recoiled in horror; the flattened eye swelled again, elastically, and, with a little earth in the corner of its gaze, it pursued him with its stare.

He understood then that he had to pick one of those living flowers; he had to, and right away. He leaned over a delicate azure eye, the timid and charming eye of a virgin, and he pulled. The peduncle resisted, and as the eye suffered, contracting, the king saw it pale and agonize; he lurched slightly, in a flight of the soul, and to his invincible disgust, he saw the fluid of the eye become clouded. With supreme effort, he tore it from the ground, no longer a bulb with its tail but a delight-ful child sixteen years old who fainted in his arms and stuck her mouth to his to thank him. Unfortunately, she was blind.

He was not greatly astonished, and he covered that fresh face, so fresh and so pure that one might have thought it that of a little girl, with kisses. He spoke to her without her listening; she was deaf. He hoped that she might speak, but she was mute. With that, quivering and arching her back amorously, she clung to him, melting into his embrace. Intoxicated by pity and tenderness, he got carried away, dissolving in tears of an unequalled suavity, which flowed from his being like a spring of sensuality.

The old woman had rapidly woken him up, shaking his shoulders.

He ground his teeth, seeing, instead of the exquisite virgin, that wrinkled face of a witch, and it would not have taken much for him to kill the guardian, but she moaned so lamentably that she thought she had done well, since he was weeping, that he turned his back on her in order to continue his dream.

Dzz! Dzz!

The king heard a large fly buzzing somewhere. It came closer, buzzing more loudly, and fled with an abrupt swerve into the corner of the room, circling the candelabras. *Why isn't that impudent old woman chasing it away?* he wondered. Suddenly, he ceased to hear the fly, but he felt a singular tickling sensation in his nasal fossae and under the skin of the nose. *Dzz! Dzz!* The vibration of the fly rumbled like a drum. Great God, what was it doing there? And although he could not see it, the king distinguished a hideous phosphoric green fly of storm and sepulcher, with its abdomen swollen with eggs.

He would have liked . . . oh, what impotent rage, not to be able to . . . !" He would certainly have the old woman impaled. And still, under his nose, almost in his brain, the fly was buzzing, exploring his utmost depths, reaching the after-palate. Damnation, now it was tickling the uvula. And the king, thus tickled, started to laugh: a convulsive and extraordinary laughter that never finished, rising in scales, making arpeggios, bounding in cascades and swelling in gurgles, twisting him in paroxysms so torturing that in the end he woke up.

The old woman, with her arms folded, was looking at him placidly, refraining carefully from interrupting such a joyful slumber. That, at least, was the reason she gave to the king.

He immediately had a bucket of quicklime brought, along with pincers and a beehive. On his instruction, the guardian of bad dreams was stripped of her garments, and in order that she should know the reality of the visions that she had not been able to foresee or dissipate in time, her legs were thrust into the lime, her eyes were plucked out and her face was coated with honey in order that the bees would eat it.

The king then made the excellent resolution never to sleep again, and the physicians prepared potions to that effect that were so efficacious that he did not close his eyes for a week, and went mad.

His successor made peace with the nixies.

THE BOAT OF PORCELAINS

WHEN the boat was constructed, the oldest of the fays said to her godson: "Look!" All three of them were standing in the grass on the edge of the bank, like great lilies. Hans Ulrich turned toward the stream.

Although it was at the source, it was as wide as a pond; over the troubled water, the smooth surface of which was gleaming in the sunlight like a bronze mirror, the boat doubled its shiny hull in the motionless glass. It had the form of one of the heavy pinnaces that descend the current with a solemn slowness, and one turns round in the evening to watch them pass silently over the fleeting route of canals and rivers. A bright varnish made the sides sparkle, and the pale green flotation line sliced it immaculately.

Hans Ulrich admired the sky, still quivering with the morning light, and his gaze went from the boat designated by the fay's finger toward the Orient, from which direction the stream flowed, through a row of tall shivering poplars. A golden mist barred the horizon, and pink clouds were floating in the pure sky.

"Look!" said the oldest of the fays. "The boat is laden. You're going to embark soon. Before the anchor is raised and the voyage commences I want to pass in review with you the riches that are asleep within the boat's flanks. My sisters and I have heaped up on the planks the most beautiful porcelains in the world.

"With such a cargo, Hans, you can become the happiest of men. if you want to be. Only make good use of your treasure. At every port of call, you'll be able to exchange the porcelains of the departure for clinking gold and silver that is good to touch. Since everything can be bought, they will also serve you to procure the pleasures and pains of life. But don't lavish your fragile treasure on all comers, for these porcelains crack; others break, and the provision will be worm away.

"In the hold there are piles of plates on which cocks are painted, with their red and blue plumes, soup tureens with round bellies strewn with naïve flowers blooming in the enamel, and brown cooking-pots the color of earth. Along the shelves between the decks we have stacked wood that bears sage mottoes inscribed on banderoles. Squat goblets are alongside fine cups, coarse faiences beside delicate ceramics that have the translucent lightness of eggshells. There are all kinds of fabrics of all provenances; Nevers spoons are rubbing shoulders with Saxe figurines, and Persian phials with Chinese vases.

"The boat is full to the brim. Merchandise is over-flowing in every corner. You have amphorae of red clay and ewers of various forms made of dazzling sandstones. They are doubtless innumerable, but remember, Hans, that once the voyage is begun you will never be able to restock *en route*. Be economical with your wealth."

Having spoke thus, the oldest of the fays, whose name composed the mysterious syllables signifying Wisdom and Resignation, gazed at Hans Ulrich. He had retained nothing of the fateful words. He was only waiting, with an extreme impatience, for the voice to shut up, at the end of a speech devoid of meaning. He was quivering with desire, and his intoxicated eyes, without seeing the laden boat or the calm stream, like a pond, were contemplating the horizon where, in the far distance, beneath the pink clouds, the fleeing water was disappearing into the golden mist.

"Adieu, Hans," said the oldest of the fays.

But without hearing her, Hans leapt recklessly into the heavy boat. He seized the mooring cable with a joyful gesture and gradually, pulling on the wet rope, brought the anchor to the surface of the water. It was covered in marine plants, and, dragging its tresses of shiny glaucous leaves, moist with droplets, he threw it against the bulwark.

"Adieu Hans! Adieu, Hans!" repeated the other two fays sadly, until silence fell.

The boat, seized by the current, had moved away gradually. Over the smooth surface of the stream, cleaving through the water-lilies and the reeds, it slid through the fluvial vegetation. It was detached from the plants of old, the dying foliage in which its hull had been plunged for a long time. And while the sad voices decreased on the bank, the plants behind it undulated like long ribbons in the clear water, agitated as if in a signal of adieu.

Hans did not see any of that. Sitting in the prow, his legs dangling, he gazed into the distance at the fresh water plunging into the mist. Although the row of tall trees, the quivering poplars that he had perceived on the bank before departing, had already been surpassed a long time ago, nothing seemed to have changed at first. It seemed to him that the boat was still immobile. The banks of the river, however, unfurled before him, with immense plains, the checkerboard of fields rising in a gentle slope all the way to the line of blue hills. Clumps of trees surged forth with the brightness of their new verdure, for it was the early days of spring. The sky had the softness of fresh satin, and over the tips of the wheat, scarcely green, white frissons passed with the breath of the breeze.

Hans kept his eyes fixed on the bend in the river on the marvelous horizon. He enjoyed neither the transparency of the air nor the purity of the water. In vain the willows, with a faint murmur, dipped their long flexible branches, on which silver leaves palpitated, into the current. In their inlets, washerwomen called out to him with laughter and pursued him with songs while deploying linen the color of snow. Hans only had eyes for the distant mist.

A prodigious city suddenly surged forth. It grew very precise, between the two banks, in a few seconds, with swarms of people, a mass of towers, steeples and domes. A thousand small boats surrounded the pinnace. It soon drew up beside the quay. Full of an extraordinary fever, Hans Ulrich linked it to the shore by means of a gangplank and, standing up, awaited the host of visitors; they came running from all directions. Middle-aged men shook his hand with a sudden enthusiasm. Old men came to sit down with him in order to give him advice, and children cocked a snook at him, while women came in and went out, admiring him with moist eyes. And because some of them smiled he distributed beautiful porcelains to them. To others he gave even more precious ones because they retained hostile and surly expressions. He exchanged for coins on which grotesque effigies were represented, without a valid motive, plates ornamented with painted cocks, florid soup tureens and brown earthenware cooking-pots.

One day, the boat departed, three quarters empty. Having found his life monotonous, Hans had embarked a troupe of traveling players. The days went by to the song of violins and flutes. Courtesans danced on the deck and the boat set about following the watercourse with heavy brocades trailing behind it.

It was now the middle of summer. The river had the appearance of a lake, burning all of a piece under the midday sun. Only a few broken rushes tore the bronze mirror, scratching the diamond-studded current with their stems. To either side, the banks unfurled with the magnificence of their changing décor. The facades of palaces alternated with dense forests, heaths and grasslands. Hans kept his eyes fixed on the bend in the river on the marvelous horizon.

However, as suntanned reapers red with sweat, leaning on their scythes, were making signs to him from the edge of a field, he dropped anchor momentarily, and in exchange for tall sheaves heavy with swollen ears he consented to sell them the ewers and amphorae. Then the boat resumed its progress and the banks filed past again.

At present there were hills charged with vines, and woods whose foliage was colored crimson, rust and gold. Autumn floated in the evening air with its splendor and its melancholy. At the front of the boat Hans now looked around. He could not tear his eyes away from the hillsides, where the roofs of villages were grouped, with their red tiles, amid the vines. Abruptly, his heart troubled by an unfamiliar sentiment, he ran to the tiller. The boat veered slowly and drew closer to the bank. Peasants were passing by on the road behind carts filled with grapes. The crop had been gathered.

Hans Ulrich shouted to them to stop, but when he wanted to buy, from the girls who were singing an old refrain loudly, their baskets overflowing with red and violet clusters, he perceived that the boat was empty. The Nevers spoons had disappeared, along with the Saxe figurines; there was no longer a single Persian phial, and the Chinese vases were in pieces. Hans only found one cracked bowl with an inscription that was still legible: *Time comes and time goes.* He held it out to the youngest but she burst into laughter and shook her head.

The boat departed again. Hans now found that it was descending too rapidly, carried away by the current. He finally understood that the river flows but the banks are immobile. They offered beneath the bleak sky the image of winter. Then, on the deserted boat, where the strolling players had died long before, turning his back to the horizon, and the black water flowing toward the rumbling of the sea. Hans looked despairingly in the direction of the Orient. But he strained his ears in vain; he did not hear the sad voices of the fays. He looked hard, but he only saw the grass of old undulating in the troubled water like a signal of adieu.

THE FOREST

THE DEAR FOREST

IF the lover with the violet eyes and changing golden hair, the one of whom I dream but have never seen, had appeared on that white, livid stormy day, my caprice would have wanted to dress her as a svelte amazon in royal blue, belted with gray leather and spurred with silver on the left leg; a plumed felt hat would have coiffed her fine head. She would be mounted on a pale chestnut mare with a mane woven in fluid silken tassels: a supple and skittish beast that walked as one dances, with a high and noble step. We would ride through the soft, fresh landscape, along a smooth stream. I would say to her:

"In the same way that our horses delight in going forth in a pair, let us play with the common reverie of our souls, and they will be in accord, even in the silence. Let us go—if that is your desire?—along this river, whose slow and inflexible mirror draws in its fluid course a watery sky and crystalline shade. Or would you prefer the plain, with its golden crops flamboyant in the sunlight, in a yellow of straw and flame? Or the mysterious and motionless emerald forest?

She would reply:

"The forest alone is in accord with my heart. The one into which we are going to plunge is profound. I know it well. It might be close to Paris and touch two towns, which are Melun and Fontainebleau, but it is solitary nevertheless. A few carriages, rare cyclists, and those poor fellows who, with their shoes suspended by a string around their necks, go barefoot from one end of France to the other, are all we risk encountering on the highway and the king's pavements. But we will not even perceive them, for see: here already are the sandy paths where gallops extend as far as the eye can see through the infinite maze of other paths, opening arches of azure and sky. From now on we can wander for hours without encountering a single living being."

I reply:

"Yes, this forest is truly strange, and beautiful by dint of solitude, silence and mystery. It has no moving water, so the birds do not sing there. It's a forest devoid of delicate little singers. One only sees black crows, magpies and the wild beasts of the air, russet birds of prey. They slake their thirst at a few sad ponds. The rain also fills a few rock pools, but very few, for where it falls the sand drinks it. However, charming beasts live in the green shadow of the beech groves and among the rocks corroded by leprous mosses; there are herds of roe deer and red deer, innumerable rabbits browsing the pink heather, inoffensive lizards and malevolent vipers."

She looks at me, smiling, with dreams in her eyes and an indefinable grace in her indolent stance, swayed by the rhythmic steps of the chestnut mare, and she says:

"Is it not singular to think"—and her hand, gloved like a musketeer's, extends the pommel of her whip toward one of the innumerable signposts that throng the forest in all directions—"that all these bizarre and charming names: Route du Faon, du Cerf, du Porte-Arquebuse, Carrefour des Vieux-Rayons, Table du Grand-Maître, Cabinet de Monseigneur, Ventes Bouchard and a hundred or a thousand others, engraved in black on white planks at the top of signposts, baptize roads without travelers, labyrinths without crowds, a city of trees, dead and absolutely deserted? For myself, I sense here a charm that I cannot express but which penetrates me. Suppose—the case has been seen—some ignorant and debilitated old man or poor woman lost in this maze of labeled roads; what anguish would those cabalistic signs, which they could not read, inflict? Has the idea never occurred to you of an accident, a dangerous fall, a stroke, or no matter what pretext, isolating you, defenseless and paralyzed on the ground. while your horse escapes and gallops away, all the way to some highway, where people will stop it unless, guided by an instinct, it returns home, nostrils flared, reins broken and stirrups swinging, to the stable? Days and nights might go by before you were found, dying or dead, in the hollow of a rock or the old leaves of past years. How that search for an absentee would lend something rare and deceptive, poignant and mysterious to all those evocative names, which, extending a black arrow beneath each name for the sake of greater clarity, all seem to be saying, in chorus; That way! Search! Search!"

"Why deny it?" I reply. "An obscure consciousness of peril sharpens the sweetness of the moment one is living. It is thus that the pleasure one has in jumping over an obstacle on a good animal is enfevering and sharp. The serenity of a blue night starred by little white diamonds draws a part of its price from the idea that an intrusive footstep is about to brush the grass, that a hostile shadow might appear in the moonlight, or simply that someone unseen might be lying in wait for you. The solitude that our waking dreams populate isn't a solitude; the echo of our soul follows us there, like footfalls on the nocturnal gravel. I love this forest, which is full of myself, which seems to be nothing but me, and only to exist for me. I love the magic that it disengages, the spell of the glaucous shade in which it bathes the solitary stroller. A mild fever stagnates in the damp underwood, where monstrous mushrooms vegetate; when one has wandered into the midst of tall, straight beeches, like the pillars of cathedrals, it is as if one were drunk; one cannot sleep well on the russet needles of pines. Sometimes, if a horse's hoof collides with subterranean roots on the high plateaux, the earth rumbles like a distant drum, and that bleak sound stirs a nostalgia within you that is as indescribable as it is inexplicable."

She resumes—and I love her violet liquid eyes in which the forest and the sky are mirrored:

"The most beautiful places are not the most familiar. There is an official majesty in conventional sites.

Administrative plaques are affixed to them, in order that no one can be unaware of them, the rubric of "artistic scene," an odiously bourgeois phrase, destined for souls that it is prudent to warn that they have a choice spectacle before them. A vague respect, a confused sentiment of nature, awakens in them then, which is numbed again as soon as they have passed the so-called "artistic" zone on the way back. Without speaking ill of consecrated places where some commercial enterprise displays various beverages for the refreshment of admiring tourists, I prefer lost solitudes, unexplored promontories, nameless ponds, enchanted expanses of vegetation under centenarian trees, where one only sees ferns and fallen pine cones."

Meanwhile, by means of a difficult climb, we reach a platform on a bed of rocks, from which the view discovers a vast and infinite accumulation of treetops, a green sea with innumerable frozen waves.

"There," I say, "is an eternal spectacle of which the heart cannot weary. A pox on the miserable agitation of cities, unhealthy ambitions, the desire to shine, the confused and horrible struggle of interests, negotiations, the bread that one snatches in the struggle, in the dust of streets worn away to the bones of the stone by the feet of millions of men. Do you not have a desire to tread virgin grass, to respire air that is not shared by innumerable mouths? How far away the life of human anthills seems when one contemplates, as we are doing, this ocean of branches, of distinct and harmonious greens, whose waves rustle, in spite of the lack of wind, with a scarcely discernible but distinct and profound murmur, the very respiration of existence."

So saying, I turned toward her.

But the lover with the violet eyes made no response, and my gaze searched for her in vain, evaporated like a wisp of mist in the sunlight.

Had I been conversing with a shadow, or with myself? Flower of my dream, born of a breath, had she vanished in a breath for no reason, as she had flourished?

For a second, I had believed in her existence; I had seen her smile beneath the amazon hat, and the harmonious pleats of her skirt falling gracefully over her gray leather thigh-boots. Had I not been in love with her delicate features and her changing golden hair? Had I not seen her flatter, with her long had, the supple neck of the chestnut mare with the braided silken mane?

Meanwhile, from the elevated viewpoint, the motionless monotony of the trees is deployed all the way to the horizon, under the white sky in which a storm weighs. And my horse, of its own accord, extends its neck between the slack reins toward the distant village and the stable.

THE ENCHANTED FOREST

To Félix Boucher[1]

"WAIT, old friend; it's full of wild anemones!"

The chestnut horse, sniffing the dry heather, stretches its long placid head between the loose reins and browses the yellow spikes of the fine grass.

Those anemones, royal violet lilies with golden hearts on short velvet stems, are worth the trouble of dismounting.

"What do you say to that, friend?"

At the familiar voice, the animal turns its neck, swollen by veins and shiny with sweat. Its bulging large black eye shows a corner of fearful white, and the forest is mirrored in the somber varnished orb of that eye, which does not see in the same way as ours and deforms everything.

"What's the matter, then?"

---

1 Presumably the landscape painter Joseph Félix Boucher (1853-1937), unless the author has mistaken the forename of the far more famous eighteenth-century rococo painter François Boucher, who was greatly admired by Edmond de Goncourt.

Anxiety of the head turned to the wind, nostrils quivering, then relaxation, forgetfulness of the fugitive sensation; and peacefully, bending its limbs, the horse shears the thin grass of a rut, chews some bark and tries to dig up the fresh shoots. Whence came its fear, the instantaneous breath that made its entire body vibrate? That's a mystery of animals, strange seers of distant things. They hear things that the human ear cannot perceive. The woodland, however, is empty: no sound of any ax felling trees, no cry of a cuckoo or a woodpecker, the one known as the carpenter bird; the wild doves aren't cooing. The forest extends silently, empty and full. Perhaps the flight of a crow darkened the earth with its wing-beat? Or a branch might have snapped.

"That's good, eh?"

Yes, it must be flavorsome to chew, that damp greenness; it's good, after dry straw, dry oats and dry hay that crackle in the teeth. Its tongue clicks, embarrassed by the bit. It's true that the verdure is desirable, all that foliage swollen by moisture, its cool acidity.

Into the saddle now; the bouquet is harvested. Flowers are rare in the forest. only near the fields does the wild mint with blue flowers flourish, with buttercups, campanulas and little wild carnations that smell like roses. These velvety anemones, of such a rich violet, have scarcely knotted a blade of grass than they close and wither.

The sinuous sandy path enters russet bushes. The woodland is pruned behind and before, everywhere; great blue days where gigantic beeches loom up, white poplars and elms. A carpet of dead leaves and yellow brushwood allows thin spikes of new greenery and pink grasses to protrude here and there.

A week ago one might have thought of the somnolence of an autumnal forest, gray and grilled. Visibly, spring has surged forth, springing, bounding and bursting in green buds, sprouting emerald fingernails and digits, launching rockets that burst and fall back in leafy rain; it is the glory of green and yellow, especially yellow. A colossal virgin lace envelops the old white and black trunks with a sculpted mesh. Thousands of beings, which are leaves and which palpitate like birds, scintillate in frissons of light. And that reeks of the flesh of wood, the blood of sap, of eternal youth.

Sharp gusts pass, cockchafers zigzag in little phosphorescent wakes, a gray lizard runs over a rock, little creatures, steel-blue, dark or milky green, glide through the undergrowth; sometimes the exquisite and feverish odor of a pond, the damp aroma of mushrooms is exhaled, sometimes the dry and resinous perfume, so penetrating, of pines. Here, a breath of musk, there, a sigh of dead heather; and everywhere, the profound breath of the young forest, a great wind of strength and new life.

The beech groves are thickening their foliage already. In their run to green, to the uniform green of summer, the ascendant and precipitant scale of blonds, faint golds, greenish sulfurs and yellows darkening by

the hour, belated things, straight and rugged ships'
masts, pillars of unfinished cathedrals, all similar, are
ignited by frail foliage, embryonic and misty in the
distance.

Going forward, treading the sandy pathways,
piercing the infinite blue arch of arbors, the foliage of
which intoxicates and harasses you delightfully, changing and monotonous waves, similar and nuanced, now
the mirage, the fever of languor, the magic of the forest
subjugates and enchants you. A wordless music, the
muted and confused soul of things, an exquisite and
perfidious spell, protects you. You no longer belong
to yourself but to her. Dispossessed of time and place,
desire and regret, there is no longer anything within
you but the instinct of wandering for hours, aimlessly,
at random, reduced to living the unique life of the
senses, the mind so floating that it is almost dissolved.

"What now, old chap?"

Look, roe deer! A supple and fearful herd, in exile.
One of them seems to be waiting, half-turned toward
us. Its tawny pelt is lustrous in the sunlight. A leap, and
it flees! And the savage heart of the old man thinks of
bounding in pursuit to the rhythm, of a gallop, amid
the fanfares of the wind, the mortal baying of a pack,
the friction of boots in stirrups, seeking to overtake a
rival, under the ardent eyes of amazons.

But no; we go on at a walking pace, very gently.
And perhaps we shall see the roe deer again, through

a thicket, aiming their velvet eyes at us, gathered in a group that might release them like an arrow from a bow, carried away by a new alarm, into the distance this time, and invisible. White rocks, tinted blue-gray, riddled with holes like sponges, reflect the sky in minuscule lakes, overflowing at present, under ruddy pines, in a bed of withered moss, slippery needles and split pine-cones. The knots of serpentine roots make the soil hunchbacked. The earth snores under the hooves, marching to a distant drum.

The chestnut has resumed his dream; had he ever quit it? His somnambulistic step rises and falls in a traced, automatic curve; the muscles of the shoulders flex under the warm hide, the neat and shiny coat. He is living the continuous dream of his soul, and that dream, or a similar one, hallucinates the rider.

Or is it all this green that is obsessive; it enters into you through a thousand pores. Is it possible to think about anything else? An attempt at consciousness breaks and scatters at each of these dendritic forms, branched and leafy, which enter into the gaze. A chaos analogous to that of a symphony in which all the instruments are perceptible rocks the waking dreamer and the marching beast with its powerful undulation. At the most, incomplete sensations suggest a desire to drink from the pools in which the face of the sky extends, flattened, in the surly brushwood dotted with yellow gorse.

*

Green fever!

It has gripped me entirely with its vague insomnia, its fluid incoherence, its shadowy frissons, its sunlit warmth, the fever of languor, the malaria of trees, the soft and sensual bewilderment of being oneself and no longer oneself, stripped of all the contingencies imposed by heredity and conventional life, forgetting what things are called and that one fills a tiny square on the social chessboard, no longer belonging to anything but primordial instinct, an effigy of the race and the species, in the nudity of a soul, which it is sufficient to feel palpitating like foliage, as animals do.

Long ago!

Ah, long ago, the eternal spell of waters and woods was more ensorcelling; the green fever was confounded with the delirium of amour. For these solitary glens, for these beech-groves where an old mystery floats, for these rocks, for these robust thickets and these circular clearings, for these stars of green paths leading into the unknown, for the gaping clefts opening over oceans of treetops and accumulations of verdure, for the old split trees and the humblest stem of grass, my adolescence swelled with desire, and I loved the forest as one loves a woman. She was utterly voluptuous, and I would have loved to embrace the white birches, to roll in the green tresses of the undergrowth, to swoon on the warm breast of the giant.

Today, the green fever has become chronic. Its fits are brief. I come to life therein. I love them for the intense and lost dream that they awaken in me, for the unformulated poetry with which the forest, impassive but so beautiful, bathes my heart in accordance with infantile chimeras. Why ask more of the forest than its mirage? Toward the Orient, all the leaves sparkle, translucent and pearling the sunlight. Golden streams makes puddles in the shorn grass. Sheets of verdure in the west are stacked in creases of shadow and sharp reliefs, in joyful shifting heaps.

A unique blond hour, reminiscence of youth and brief springtimes: tomorrow the forest will be all the same green, and the spirit will blaze over that familiar splendor.

There are silver reflections on the clumps of grass. Wild pigeons are cooing in soft little sobs. The enchanted forest is vibrant with sound. Dear lie of life, beautiful lure of things!

"At the gallop, old comrade! Let's break the spell by means of a simulation of action. It's necessary to shake off this fever, which entwines and devours.

"Homeward!"

THE PASSING MOMENT

*C*HARACTERS: *Prince Avril. Prince Mai, Princesse Rose; the four fays.*
Scene: A forest in spring.

The grass in the clearing is scintillating with dew. The sky is a vivid blue. The new leaves, freshly emerald, are quivering in the morning sunlight. In the mist floating at the level of the path, with her indecisive robe, the fay of spring appears.

THE FAY OF SPRING: A few more days and butterflies the color of sulfur will be circling in the warm air. In the distance, the sap is palpitating. The mobile foliage of the birches is trembling at the end of the flexible branches, with a reflection of snow. A penetrating perfume is emerging from the moist earth, and the black trunks of the most rugged oaks are rustling, enveloped by bright lace.

She approaches a spring, gushing between two mossy rocks under tall poplars. The mirror of the fresh water is just large enough for the fay to be reflected therein.

THE FAY: So, the mysterious life of things does not pause for a minute. The hard ice, in which nothing has appeared for long months, has gradually turned to silver liquid. Once again, I can lean my changing face over it. Everywhere, on the multitudinous stems of diamond-studded grass, in the heart of the trees, in the thickets and the forest, a frisson is passing. It is life, the mysterious life of things! They are transforming and renewing. The gleaming buds contain entire foliages, and the buds themselves, before the sap awakens, are asleep in the dry fibers of bark. For everything is accomplished in accordance with immutable laws, to an eternal rhythm. Everything is modified, but nothing changes.

At the end of a pathway, far away, two strollers appear. They are walking slowly, hand in hand. They are not saying anything, but they are looking at one another with ecstatic smiles. Nothing else exists for them: the path that they are following, the morning, or the forest.

THE FAY: There! Lovers! Shall I hide? What's the point? Can those fools see anything except one another?

PRINCE AVRIL: How can I say what I feel? Why even try? There are moments when all speech seems vain, when one truly only hears in the depths of the soul, by virtue of silence. But there are other moments when joy bursts forth. One would like to find words, cries . . .

PRINCESSE ROSE: Are we not always going to walk like this.

PRINCE AVRIL: Such moments never end. Their memory perfumes life.

PRINCESSE ROSE: I love you!

PRICE AVRIL: Oh, this moment, this divine moment, if you knew how long I have waited for it! How many times, with a heavy heart, I have followed this same path aimlessly! I was intoxicated by love. I proclaimed it to the air, to the trees, to the spring . . .

PRINCESSE ROSE: Look at my pretty bouquet: a branch from an almond tree and wild violets.

PRINCE AVRIL: Don't shake it; the petals are falling.

PRINCESSE ROSE: The almond trees will flower again. Will you still love me?

PRINCE AVRIL: Can the shadow of the oak tree quit its foot?

PRINCESSE ROSE: Then let time go by, my prince; for I shall always love you . . .

They have traversed the clearing, and they go into the path that plunges into the thicket on the far side and draw away, absorbed in their dream. The trodden grass stands up again. It is as if no one had passed that way. Silence reigns again. Only an oriole, swinging on a supple branch, is whistling.

And time goes by.

THE FAY OF SPRING: Gradually, the emerald of the new leaves has faded. In the treetops, they undulate with a graver murmur, and when the sun strikes them they design a mobile net on the ground, with a mesh of light and shadow. The warm earth exhales an odor of honey. Flies buzz. Already the wheat is rising, the field are bristling with hard ears. Cornflowers and poppies are abundant.

She looks into the mirror of the spring.

My grace is fading. My robe of mist is evaporating. Summer is coming. My sister is on the move.

Insensibly, the décor has changed. Large, somnolent clouds are motionless in the dark blue sky. At the foot of the mossy rock, between the poplars, the fay of summer has just appeared. She is clad in white. The torsade of her long hair is falling over her bare shoulders. She sits down next to her languishing sister and they both dangle their white feet in the cold water.

THE FAY OF SUMMER: While the crops grow in full furrows it's pleasant to lie down, far from the sun. Thanks to you, good sister, I'm not fatigued by the route traced in slow steps. I can savor the freshness of the shade. In the distance, the universal toil is being accomplished. The fruits are ripening by themselves. In the orchards the warm plums are falling with a dull sound. Soon, the scythes will be whistling through the gold of straw; the sheaves will be bound, the ricks erected. Meanwhile, lying in the grass, I can hear the axles of carts squeaking.

Silently, they listen to the distant rumor of the day dwindle away. Golden dust floats at the level of the thickets. The trees of the clearing are gradually tinted with crimson, violet and yellow. Invisible October has touched the foliage with its rusty finger. A faint breeze stirs it. Muted fanfares of hunting horns murmur.

THE FAY OF SUMMER: Our sister is on the move. She's approaching soundlessly over the moss.

Autumn is certainly not far away when the melancholy fanfare of horns resounds.

At the end of the path, in the distance, a hunt is galloping, with its spotted dogs. One by one, in the clearing, the leaves turn. Several fall into the spring, where circular ripples expand. And the fay of autumn, arrived from who knows where, leans over the rust-colored water with her sisters.

THE FAY OF AUTUMN: On the surface of the trouble water, my sisters, my face is confounded with yours, for I summarize both of you. I ally the grace of spring with the splendor of summer. Already the heavy clusters are falling, in woven baskets into the bellies of barrels. The sun, which does not want to die, is radiating with a supreme brightness at the end of long days, but the hours are falling, one after another; and through the grand avenues they are making their monotonous rounds with the leaves. Our sister is on the way.

A sharp frisson runs through the woods. The sky is covered. The clouds pursue one another, extending nets of rain. The three sisters shiver on the bare earth. Slowly, the daylight fades and the chill increases. Sparse snowflakes flutter. Bent double, the fay of winter, a little old woman, appears.

THE FAY OF WINTER: Let's huddle together, my sisters, on the edge of the opaque spring.

THE OTHER THREE FAYS: In vain, alas, we incline our image toward her. Nothing is reflected by the hard water, a mirror without silver. Do we still exist?

THE FAY OF WINTER: We exist eternally. The snow is dying in silent flakes, but it plaits time as it does so. It drapes everything with an immense shroud; its glacial level extends; but under the earth the future crop is elaborating, and in gusts, above the dazzling carpet, the forest sways its thousand black skeletons, in which the renewal is dormant.

And time passes, time passes.

But not for one minute does the mysterious life of things stop. They are transformed, they are renewed, with the consequence that one day, the snow has melted and the sky is a vivid blue. Spring has returned; and the new leaves, freshly emerald, quiver in the morning sunlight. And the four fays, invisible but present, allow a flap of their indecisive robes to trail in the mist that floats at the level of the path.

Someone is coming.

It is Prince Avril. He is alone, as pale as a wounded man. He is respiring a bouquet of almond flowers and wild violets. At the foot of the mossy rock, he leans against one of the tall poplars and sobs.

Meanwhile, at the end of the path, two strollers appear. They are walking hand in hand. It is Princesse Rose and Prince Mai. Clad in green, like Prince Avril, the latter resembles his older brother. The lovers are not saying anything to one another, but they are looking at one another with ecstatic smiles. Nothing else exists for them: not the path they are fooling, the morning or the forest. They pass close to Prince Avril without seeing him.

PRINCESSE ROSE: Tell me that we're going to walk like this endlessly.

PRINCE MAI: Can one forget such moments? They are prolonged eternally.

PRINCESSE ROSE: Look at my pretty bouquet: a hawthorn branch with eglantine roses.

PRINCE MAI: They shed their petals quickly.

PRINCESSE ROSE: They'll flower again. Will you still love me?

PRINE MAI: For as long as there are eglantine roses.

PRINCESSE ROSE: Let time go by then, my prince, For myself, I shall always love you . . . .

They traverse the clearing, and they both draw away along the path that plunges into the thicket. The grass, scarcely trodden down, stands up again. Silence reigns once more. Only an oriole whistles as it swings on a supple branch.

Killed by thrusts of memory, Prince Avril lies on the edge of the spring. But the forest pursues its great life; the sap palpitates in the distance, over the inert body, on the multitudinous diamond-studded stems, in the heart of the trees, through the new verdure, a frisson passes, and in the mist where their indecisive robes float, the silent round of the four eternal sisters, the immutable fays with changing faces, goes on.

YPÉRION

THE MANNEQUIN

To Armand Point[1]

BERLURON said to Malavelle: "I'm giving you Ypérion; he'd encumber me in my voyage. Take him, he's yours. But have the regard for him that is owed to a human effigy. That natural-sized wooden androgyne with articulated limbs and a noble and smiling face is inhabited, be sure of it, by an obscure soul. Ypérion has, confusedly, a notion of good and evil, a love of farces, a genius for complication and a tendency to obscene things. He knows how to deploy, with a motionless gesture, the eloquence of a mine; no fire in a living tableau can match him for the rigidity and precision of a pose. Make a friend of Ypérion; he's worthy of it. Be familiar with him, but don't allow your

---

1 The painter Armand Point (c1869-1932), born in Algiers, whose early work often reproduced scenes of that city. Later in his career he became a Symbolist, associated with the Salon de la Rose + Croix, and he symbolized his rejection of Naturalism with a poster for the salon depicting Perseus holding aloft the head of Émile Zola instead of that of Medusa.

entourage to abuse his complaisance. Docile as he is, rancor is not unknown to him. Our friend Vermusse knows that now. He never came into this studio without putting his fist under Ypérion's nose; he insulted him with disgust. He pulled his ears, kneed him in the groin, and one day, when he was drunk, he wanted to introduce a red-hot poker into his wooden fundament. How Ypéerion avenged himself, you know. Crouched on the stairs, he tripped Vermusse as he went past; our friend tumbled down the steps and picked up a sprain that twisted his foot. The spectacle was so painful to Vermusse's mistress that she couldn't bear it. She quit her lover to cheat on him, the same evening, with a Bolivian. Don't attract similar misfortunes. And to conciliate Ypérion's good graces, so that he'll be mild in his relations and constant in his attitudes, don't hesitate, I assure you, to tickle his neck, his armpits, his elbows, his kneecaps and—to call things by their name—what takes the place of his absence of sex, with a feather moistened with sweet almond oil!"

Impressed, Malavelle replied: "I'll take him with me, then. The country air will do him good. He's a little thin and dry. When we work together I'll install him in my garden under my big cherry tree. The birds will be afraid of him."

Berluron shook the ash from his pipe and approached Ypérion; he contemplated the mannequin with an affectionate gaze—who, stark naked and leaning against the wall, resembled a thin brown Egyptian in the process of being mummified.

"Poor old chap," he said. "I shan't see you again, then. Believe it or not Malavelle, it isn't without regret that I'm separating from such a companion. He was the household god of this studio. He's seen it in all colors. He knows that Irma has a beauty spot on which she sits down and that the corn on Bibiche's foot resists all the inventions of science. Many times, when supper was lacking, Ypérion regaled us with one of those ludicrous scenes whose bad taste is only excused by their whimsicality. I don't have the patience, Malavelle, to tell you all of them. You can't, however, be unaware of the delightful fear—I mean delightful for us, myself and my dear companion Minette—that Hypérion inspires in the wife of our landlord when, in a chemise and on the point of going to bed, alerted by the desperate barking of her roquet, she leans over, candle in hand, to look under the bed, and perceives an artilleryman with his shako and saber, doubtless waiting there for her to go to sleep in order to violate her with an energy that would not have excluded all gentleness."

Malavelle shook his head obligingly, and said: "She's good!"

"No," said Berluron, "she's weak. But here's a better one. One evening, when Ypériod was melancholy and sprawling, in order to shake him up, we took him to various brasseries and to a ballroom; but monsieur was lugubrious; he was restless on the banquettes, he looked at us disdainfully, and people began to make fun of us and the corpse that we were dragging around. 'Very well,' I say. 'You don't want to have fun with your brethren. Get up! Go back to the house. Hey, Coachman!' and I hail a cab. We shove the comrade inside, shut the door and shot my address. Then, shaking an imaginary hand, we shout: 'Bonsoir! Until tomorrow!' And the coachman, who has only seen smoke, pulls away, carrying our man. We split our sides, writhing with laughter, agitated by such spasms that we have to lie down in the sidewalk—yes, we split our sides at the thought of the face the coachman would pull when he shakes his client, cursing the five hundred devils, waking my concierge and the whole house, rousing the entire quarter. Pure vision, Malavelle, dream, inanity, bubble of air! None of that happened. The coachman, unmoved, asked my concierge: 'Do you know this individual?' 'Of course,' the concierge replies, 'that's Monsieur Ypérion. He makes excursions like that occasionally. I'll pay the fare!' And when I come back the next morning, Ypérion is mounting guard on my landing. The milk pail which a cunning milkman has just filled with a liquid, blue-tinted on top like laundry liquid, and white underneath like boiled chalk and calf-brains, is swinging on his arm. He has a sardonic and contemptuous expression. That cost me a hundred sous, Malavelle, and Minette reproached me for it—what am I saying?—she still reproaches me for it. It was seven years ago. But a woman, unlike a wasp, doesn't leave her sting in the wound and doesn't die of the prick she's just given you!"

Having let that remark fall, in a thoughtful tone, Berluron gazed into the distance vaguely.

"An excellent joke to play is this: drape Ypérion in a woman's dress; lay him down on a sofa facing the wall, wrap his head in a mantilla and his feet in a shawl, and when a guest or a visitor arrives, say: 'Shh!' and point to the sleeping and suffering form, whispering: 'My good friend is ill, a bad neuralgia; if you don't mind, we'll talk downstairs.' If, by chance, the visitor—it can happen; admit it, you suspected as much—is in love with your mistress, leaving him alone with that double will be an irrefutable and Machiavellian proof. Embarrassed at first, he'll stifle a slight cough, walk on tiptoe, then, emboldened, making the furniture creak, he'll call to the charming and criminally coveted creature in a low voice. What will your joy be, behind the door, if you see him launch into a verbose declaration and tuck up the skirts of the sleeper impudently! Imagine his subsequent consternation, his furious and vexed bafflement!"

"I'll do it to Crikosch," said Malavelle. "I'll do it tomorrow; I know that he fancies my wife."

And at that prospect, he opens one eye wide and shuts the other, twisting his mouth frightfully into a hen's backside, which is the laughter of clowns and buffoons.

"Why not," said Berluron, "one evening when you're partying at home, when fruits, beer, iced water and white wine are exercising a refreshing and treacherous influence, enclose Ypérion in the redoubt that you know? A semi-darkness will envelop him and, his forehead supported by one hand, in a pose full of gravity and expectation, put a crumpled piece of paper in his other hand. The guests, one after another, will push the door and close it again precipitately, babbling; 'Oh, pardon me!' and they'll return to the rooms of the party with a retained and contracted expression. In truth Malavelle, I assure you, Ypérion will be a source of ineffable joys for you. You can vary them infinitely, and my memory will remain dear to you, associated as it will be with transformations as numerous as those of Proteus, which this wooden sage will incarnate. Now, if you believe me, take him away. It's time. Go! I've seen enough of you. And you, Ypérion, adieu!"

An emotion passed through Berluron's voice; he leaned toward Malavelle's ear

"When I return, you can tell me what you've done with him. Oh, the rogue! There's one who won't be bored in life!"

He added: "Play the trick of the sleeping woman on Crikosch. That and the coup of the staircase, Vermusse's sprain—they're the two best ones I know!"

YPÉRION'S ADVENTURES

IT was in the garden of the painter Berluron on the bank of the Marne. He was finishing his pope, sitting before his easel, while little Merlette, Mère Merleau's daughter, an odd girl, vicious and ingenuous, took off her petticoat and her stockings behind a little canvas screen, in order to place them in the open air.

She showed herself, very thin, with very white skin, but a tanned face, and hands that she brought back, with a pretty gesture over her barely-prominent breasts.

"Have they grown, M'sieu Berluron, since the other day?"

She kicked the dog, Charlemagne, which had come to sniff her.

"There's a senator!" she said, indignantly.

"Here!" the painter whistled. Charlemagne returned, crawling, and received a slap on the nose.

"Lie down there!"

"M'sieu Berluron, you're putting me in your painting, aren't you?" asked Merlette.

"Which part, Fleur-de-Lin?"

He called her that because she had eyes of a very pure blue, so suave that one would have given her to the good God without confession—which did not prevent her from being caught with the son of the wheelwright and receiving a fine scolding served up by her father, the corn-chandler, Thomas Grouin, Merleau's lover.

"Heads, M'sieur Berluron. Oh, I'd like to have one like my sister, la Jarousse! She's got one! So . . ."

A celestial vision passed in her eye.

"What does she do, your sister?"

"She's with a marquis; she has thirty-six chemises and plumed hats. Saving your respect," she added, with a certain pride, "she's a maintained demoiselle."

"On her back," muttered Berluron, in a low voice, almost losing his temper. Little Merlette laughed. She had understood.

"Oh, when I'm grown up . . . !" she sighed.

"What will you do, Fleur-de-Lin?"

"I'll be someone rich, M'sieu Berluron. It's not for dogs that there are fine carriages. You see, I'll go to the theater every evening and eat sugared dishes. Look! There are birds perching on M'sieu Ypérion. Truly, if I weren't so afraid of Thomas Grouin . . . !"

Berluron glanced at the life-sized mannequin that, clad in the coat of a garde-française and a flannel skirt, armed with a horse-syringe, was mounting guard between three cherry-trees, his wooden head protected from the sun by a bicorn hat made from a newspaper.

"Ypérion's bored," he said. "He's recounting his amours with Princesse Cascatelle to the birds."

"His amours! Oh la la! Of dead wood!"

Berluron became grave.

"Why shouldn't he have any? Ypérion, such as you see him, has traveled in marvelous lands and his adventures are extraordinary. He's no less alive for being wood, and very alive. I concede that he's a little desiccated. The hour isn't far off when he'll grow leaves all spring and give us pears in the autumn. Doubtless he might, not having been purged for a long time, be prey to a slightly stubborn constipation. Remember, however, that his little gifts aren't to be scorned, if I can judge by the fuss you make of them."

A few days before, little Merlette had found Ypérion in the studio, modestly crouched on a chamber pot in which little black balls were accumulated, smelly goat droppings in appearance but excellent licorice in reality. She laughed heartily at the memory and said: "All that's jokes, M'sieu Berluron."

He seemed quite annoyed.

"You don't believe in anything, then? You have no religion?"

That seemed to impress her.

"Oh, how can you say that?" she cried. "I believe lots of things. If you put your stockings on backwards, you'll receive a visit, Everyone knows that there are werewolves. Spit three times in a circle and say: 'Come in, Jean de Satan' and the devil appears to you. He has the backside of a billy-goat and fiery eyes, with horns. Spill salt on the tablecloth and bad luck will overtake you. You can cure burns with the bile of a leech."

She became pensive, and said in a lower voice: "The dead come back to grab you by the feet. One can cast spells on cows, and even on people. La Caillasse's aunt died of it; she swelled and swelled and then her belly burst. What did she have inside? A trefoil that a sorcerer had chewed."

"Good," said Berluron. "Since that's the way it is, why do you refuse to believe in the adventures of Ypérion? Haven't you seen more extraordinary things? The other day, when I painted a pâté on my canvas, you didn't want to believe that it was sufficient to put it in the oven for it really to cook. What happened? I sent the porter to the kitchen and a few minutes later you came back to open the oven. What did you see, and by means of what spell? An excellent warm pâté, assuredly the same one, of which you ate your share greedily."

"Get away, M'sieu Beluron, get away!" said little Merlette, resignedly. "Oh, you can catch anyone out, you!"

"Since that's the way it is, you'll never know the story of Ypériion's amours with Princesse Cascatelle."

"Tell me, I beg you; look, my arm's all stiff; that will occupy me while I listen!"

"No, no, quit the pose if you're tired. No story, if one won't believe it."

"M'sieu Berluron!"

"Oh, I'm a liar? Oh, Ypérion isn't made of licorice pastilles? Oh, the pâté I painted wasn't cooked in the oven? Oh, Ypérion didn't abduct the daughter of the Great Turk and she didn't have golden hair and silver fingernails? Good, good!"

"M'sieu Berluron, I'll believe anything you wish. Go on, I like your stories better than the stupid things that Monsieur Maclou, the beadle, wants to tell me in the corner. He's another one, the senator!"

"Fleur-de-Lin, that's the second time you've employed that vocable, to which you seem to attribute a meaning that Bescherelle and Littré haven't yet consecrated, so far as I know."

But Fleur-de-Lin refused positively to give the slightest explanation.

"Tell the story, M'sieu Berluron!"

"Well, it's necessary to tell you, first, that Ypérion . . . It was on an admirable summer night; the moon was spreading a silver wake over the waves. Princesse Cascatelle was smoking her pope on the terrace. That pipe, Fleur-de-Lin, was called a narghile, and from its receptacle and its tube a snake was coiling, resembling closely the mysterious instrument that astonished your ignorance so much when you perceived it for the first time in the house of my landlady, Madame Rissolet."[1]

"She puts it, saving your respect, elsewhere than in her nose," said Little Merlette.

"Don't conclude recklessly that the one whose perfumed amber tip Princesse Cascatelle carried was put anywhere else than between her rosy lips. The princess . . . oh, my word, how beautiful she was! Have I told you that she had golden hair and silver fingernails?

---

1 The "instrument" in question, which could not decently be named in print, would have been easily recognizable by contemporary readers as a vaginal douche, the most common method of contraception employed by fashionable Parisiennes at the time.

Good. Her hair and fingernails grew so quickly in one night that they were forced to file them every morning; you can understand that they collected the silver and gold dust very carefully. When Ypérion came to Stamboul, the princess possessed fifty leather sacks of it, which were her dowry. In fact, Cascatelle only had one eye; the other had fallen into the lake while she was bathing, one day when she has extracted it from its orbit distractedly, and was playing cup-and-ball with it. But what splendor there was in the eye that remained! It was so bright . . ."

A bell rang and Charlemagne, barked, cutting off the sentence.

"Continued in the next issue. Get dressed, Fleur-de-Lin. That's enough for today.

"Oh, M'sieu Berluron, what a joker you are," said little Merlette. "There's no bigger joker than you!"

She disappeared behind the canvas screen, hopping like a white rabbit, and suddenly, showing her hempen hair and flax-blue eyes, said: "Doesn't alter the fact, M'sieur Berluron, that you're the only one I trust. At least you respect people. Why, it's gone! Hey, Charlemagne! Stop, thief! He's taken my chemise, M'sieu Berluron. Dirty dog, will you bring it back! Oh! Oh!"

But Charlemagne ran to carry it to Ypérion, who, scandalized, fell with all his weight on his back, attesting once again to the supernatural and diabolical life by which he was animated, and which was always accompanied, in that stiff gentleman, by an appropriate decisiveness.

A PARTIAL LIST OF SNUGGLY BOOKS

ETHEL ARCHER *The Hieroglyph*
ETHEL ARCHER *Phantasy and Other Poems*
ETHEL ARCHER *The Whirlpool*
G. ALBERT AURIER *Elsewhere and Other Stories*
CHARLES BARBARA *My Lunatic Asylum*
S. HENRY BERTHOUD *Misanthropic Tales*
LÉON BLOY *The Tarantulas' Parlor and Other Unkind Tales*
ÉLÉMIR BOURGES *The Twilight of the Gods*
CYRIEL BUYSSE *The Aunts*
JAMES CHAMPAGNE *Harlem Smoke*
FÉLICIEN CHAMPSAUR *The Latin Orgy*
BRENDAN CONNELL *The Translation of Father Torturo*
BRENDAN CONNELL *Unofficial History of Pi Wei*
BRENDAN CONNELL (editor)
   The Zinzolin Book of Occult fiction
RAFAELA CONTRERAS *The Turquoise Ring and Other Stories*
DANIEL CORRICK (editor)
   Ghosts and Robbers: An Anthology of German Gothic Fiction
ADOLFO COUVE *When I Think of My Missing Head*
QUENTIN S. CRISP *Aiaigasa*
LUCIE DELARUE-MARDRUS *The Last Siren and Other Stories*
LADY DILKE *The Outcast Spirit and Other Stories*
CATHERINE DOUSTEYSSIER-KHOZE
   The Beauty of the Death Cap
ÉDOUARD DUJARDIN *Hauntings*
BERIT ELLINGSEN *Now We Can See the Moon*
ERCKMANN-CHATRIAN *A Malediction*
ALPHONSE ESQUIROS *The Enchanted Castle*
ENRIQUE GÓMEZ CARRILLO *Sentimental Stories*
DELPHI FABRICE *Flowers of Ether*
DELPHI FABRICE *The Red Sorcerer*
DELPHI FABRICE *The Red Spider*
BENJAMIN GASTINEAU *The Reign of Satan*
EDMOND AND JULES DE GONCOURT *Manette Salomon*
REMY DE GOURMONT *From a Faraway Land*
REMY DE GOURMONT *Morose Vignettes*
GUIDO GOZZANO *Alcina and Other Stories*
GUSTAVE GUICHES *The Modesty of Sodom*

JEAN RICHEPIN *The Bull-Man and the Grasshopper*
FREDERICK ROLFE (**Baron Corvo**) *Amico di Sandro*
JASON ROLFE *An Archive of Human Nonsense*
ARNAUD RYKNER *The Last Train*
LEOPOLD VON SACHER-MASOCH
    The Black Gondola and Other Stories
MARCEL SCHWOB *The Assassins and Other Stories*
MARCEL SCHWOB *Double Heart*
CHRISTIAN HEINRICH SPIESS *The Dwarf of Westerbourg*
BRIAN STABLEFORD (**editor**)
    Decadence and Symbolism: A Showcase Anthology
BRIAN STABLEFORD (**editor**) *The Snuggly Satyricon*
BRIAN STABLEFORD (**editor**) *The Snuggly Satanicon*
BRIAN STABLEFORD *Spirits of the Vasty Deep*
COUNT ERIC STENBOCK *The Shadow of Death*
COUNT ERIC STENBOCK *Studies of Death*
MONTAGUE SUMMERS *The Bride of Christ and Other Fictions*
MONTAGUE SUMMERS *Six Ghost Stories*
ALICE TÉLOT *The Inn of Tears*
GILBERT-AUGUSTIN THIERRY *The Blonde Tress and The Mask*
GILBERT-AUGUSTIN THIERRY *Reincarnation and Redemption*
DOUGLAS THOMPSON *The Fallen West*
TOADHOUSE *Gone Fishing with Samy Rosenstock*
TOADHOUSE *Living and Dying in a Mind Field*
TOADHOUSE *What Makes the Wave Break?*
LÉO TRÉZENIK *The Confession of a Madman*
LÉO TRÉZENIK *Decadent Prose Pieces*
RUGGERO VASARI *Raun*
ILARIE VORONCA *The Confession of a False Soul*
ILARIE VORONCA *The Key to Reality*
JANE DE LA VAUDÈRE *The Demi-Sexes and The Androgynes*
AUGUSTE VILLIERS DE L'ISLE-ADAM *Isis*
RENÉE VIVIEN AND HÉLÈNE DE ZUYLEN DE NYEVELT
    Faustina and Other Stories
RENÉE VIVIEN *Lilith's Legacy*
RENÉE VIVIEN *A Woman Appeared to Me*
ILARIE VORONCA *The Confession of a False Soul*
ILARIE VORONCA *The Key to Reality*
TERESA WILMS MONTT *In the Stillness of Marble*
TERESA WILMS MONTT *Sentimental Doubts*
KAREL VAN DE WOESTIJNE *The Dying Peasant*